The Great
Fairy Tale Classics

TORMONT

**ILLUSTRATED BY TONY WOLF/PIERO CATTANEO
TEXT BY PETER HOLEINONE**

First published by DAMI EDITORE, ITALY
This edition published by :
TORMONT PUBLICATIONS INC.
338 St. Antoine St. East
Montreal, Quebec, Canada

ISBN 2-921171-28-7
Printed in Canada

THE GREAT FAIRY TALE CLASSICS

CONTENTS

4

Once upon a time . . .

. . . a little girl called Snow White was abandoned in the forest by her wicked stepmother. By chance, she met seven dwarfs, and this story is all about them . . .

SNOW WHITE AND THE SEVEN DWARFS

Once upon a time . . . in a great castle, a Prince's daughter grew up happy and contented, in spite of a jealous stepmother. She was very pretty, with blue eyes and long black hair. Her skin was delicate and fair, and so she was called Snow White. Everyone was quite sure she would become very beautiful. Though her stepmother was a wicked woman, she too was very beautiful, and the magic mirror told her this every day, whenever she asked it.

"Mirror, mirror on the wall, who is the loveliest lady in the land?" The reply was always; "You are, your Majesty," until the dreadful day when she heard it say, "Snow White is the loveliest in the land." The stepmother was furious and, wild with jealousy, began plotting to get rid of her rival. Calling one of her trusty servants, she bribed him with a rich reward to take Snow White into the forest, far away from the Castle. Then, unseen, he was to put her to death. The greedy servant, attracted to the reward, agreed to do this deed, and he led the innocent little girl away. However, when they came to the fatal spot, the man's courage failed him and, leaving Snow White sitting beside a tree, he mumbled an excuse and ran off. Snow White was all alone in the forest.

Night came, but the servant did not return. Snow White, alone in the dark forest, began to cry bitterly. She thought she could feel terrible eyes spying on her, and she heard strange sounds and rustlings that made her heart thump. At last, overcome by tiredness, she fell asleep curled under a tree.

Snow White slept fitfully, wakening from time to time with a start and staring into the darkness round her. Several times, she thought she felt something, or somebody touch her as she slept.

At last, dawn woke the forest to the song of the birds, and Snow White too, awoke. A whole world was stirring to life and the little girl was glad to see how silly her fears had been. However, the thick trees were like a wall round her, and as she tried to find out where she was, she came upon a path. She walked along it, hopefully. On she walked till she came to a clearing. There stood a strange cottage, with a tiny door, tiny windows and a tiny chimney pot. Everything about the cottage was much tinier than it ought to be. Snow White pushed the door open.

"I wonder who lives here?" she said to herself, peeping round the kitchen. "What tiny plates! And spoons! There must be seven of them, the table's laid for seven people." Upstairs was a bedroom with seven neat little beds. Going back to the kitchen, Snow White had an idea.

"I'll make them something to eat. When they come home, they'll be glad to find a meal ready." Towards dusk, seven tiny men marched homewards singing. But when they opened the door, to their surprise they found a bowl of hot steaming soup on the table, and the whole house spick and span. Upstairs was Snow White, fast asleep on one of the beds. The chief dwarf prodded her gently.

"Who are you?" he asked. Snow White told them her sad story, and tears sprang to the dwarfs' eyes. Then one of them said, as he noisily blew his nose:

"Stay here with us!"

"Hooray! Hooray!" they cheered, dancing joyfully round the little girl. The dwarfs said to Snow White:

"You can live here and tend to the house while we're down the mine. Don't worry about your stepmother leaving you in the forest. We love you and *we'll* take care of you!" Snow White gratefully accepted their hospitality, and next morning the dwarfs set off for work. But they warned Snow White not to open the door to strangers.

Meanwhile, the servant had returned to the castle, with the heart of a roe deer. He gave it to the cruel stepmother, telling her it belonged to Snow White, so that he could claim the reward. Highly pleased, the stepmother turned again to the magic mirror. But her hopes were dashed, for the mirror replied: "The loveliest in the land is still Snow White, who lives in the seven dwarfs' cottage, down in the forest." The stepmother was beside herself with rage.

"She must die! She must die!" she screamed. Disguising herself as an old peasant woman, she put a poisoned apple with the others in her basket. Then, taking the quickest way into the forest, she crossed the swamp at the edge of the trees. She reached the bank unseen, just as Snow White stood waving goodbye to the seven dwarfs on their way to the mine.

Snow White was in the kitchen when she heard the sound at the door: KNOCK! KNOCK!

"Who's there?" she called suspiciously, remembering the dwarfs' advice.

"I'm an old peasant woman selling apples," came the reply.

"I don't need any apples, thank you," she replied.

"But they are beautiful apples and ever so juicy!" said the velvety voice from outside the door.

"I'm not supposed to open the door to anyone," said the little girl, who was reluctant to disobey her friends.

"And quite right too! Good girl! If you promised not to open up to strangers, then of course you can't buy. You *are* a good girl indeed!" Then the old woman went on.

"And as a reward for being good, I'm going to make you a gift of one of my apples!" Without a further thought, Snow White opened the door just a tiny crack, to take the apple.

"There! Now isn't that a nice apple?" Snow White bit into the fruit, and as she did, fell to the ground in a faint: the effect of the terrible poison left her lifeless instantaneously.

Now chuckling evilly, the wicked stepmother hurried off. But as she ran back across the swamp, she tripped and fell into the quicksand. No one heard her cries for help, and she disappeared without a trace.

Meanwhile, the dwarfs came out of the mine to find the sky had grown dark and stormy. Loud thunder echoed through the valleys and streaks of lightning ripped the sky. Worried about Snow White, they ran as quickly as they could down the mountain to the cottage.

There they found Snow White, lying still and lifeless, the poisoned apple by her side. They did their best to bring her round, but it was no use.

They wept and wept for a long time. Then they laid her on a bed of rose petals, carried her into the forest and put her in a crystal coffin.

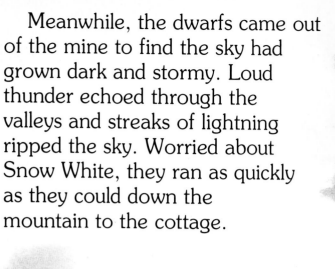

Each day they laid a flower there.

Then one evening, they discovered a strange young man admiring Snow White's lovely face through the glass. After listening to the story, the Prince (for he was a prince!) made a suggestion.

"If you allow me to take her to the Castle, I'll call in famous doctors to waken her from this peculiar sleep. She's so lovely . . . I'd love to kiss her. . . !" He did, and as though by magic, the Prince's kiss broke the spell. To everyone's astonishment, Snow White opened her eyes. She had amazingly come back to life! Now in love, the Prince asked Snow White to marry him, and the dwarfs reluctantly had to say goodbye to Snow White.

From that day on, Snow White lived happily in a great castle. But from time to time, she was drawn back to visit the little cottage down in the forest.

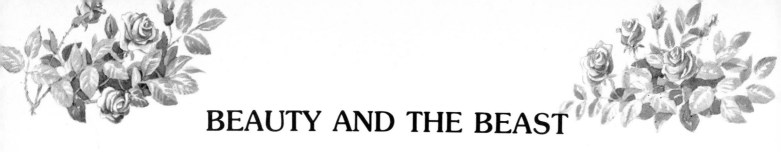

BEAUTY AND THE BEAST

Once upon a time . . . as a merchant set off for market, he asked each of his three daughters what she would like as a present on his return. The first daughter wanted a brocade dress, the second a pearl necklace, but the third, whose name was Beauty, the youngest, prettiest and sweetest of them all, said to her father:

"All I'd like is a rose you've picked specially for me!"

When the merchant had finished his business, he set off for home. However, a sudden storm blew up, and his horse could hardly make headway in the howling gale. Cold and weary, the merchant had lost all hope of reaching an inn when he suddenly noticed a bright light shining in the middle of a wood. As he drew near, he saw that it was a castle, bathed in light.

"I hope I'll find shelter there for the night," he said to himself. When he reached the door, he saw it was open, but though he shouted, nobody came to greet him. Plucking up courage, he went inside, still calling out to attract attention. On a table in the main hall, a splendid dinner lay already served. The merchant lingered, still shouting for the owner of the castle. But no one came, and so the starving merchant sat down to a hearty meal.

Overcome by curiosity, he ventured upstairs, where the corridor led into magnificent rooms and halls. A fire crackled in the first room and a soft bed looked very inviting. It was now late, and the merchant could not resist. He lay down on the bed and fell fast asleep. When he woke next morning, an unknown hand had placed a mug of steaming coffee and some fruit by his bedside.

The merchant had breakfast and after tidying himself up, went downstairs to thank his generous host. But, as on the evening before, there was nobody in sight. Shaking his head in wonder at the strangeness of it all, he went towards the garden where he had left his horse, tethered to a tree. Suddenly, a large rose bush caught his eye.

Remembering his promise to Beauty, he bent down to pick a rose. Instantly, out of the rose garden, sprang a horrible beast, wearing splendid clothes. Two bloodshot eyes, gleaming angrily, glared at him and a deep, terrifying voice growled: "Ungrateful man! I gave you shelter, you ate at my table and slept in my own bed, but now all the thanks I get is the theft of my favourite flowers! I shall put you to death for this slight!" Trembling with fear, the merchant fell on his knees before the Beast.

"Forgive me! Forgive me! Don't kill me! I'll do anything you say! The rose wasn't for me, it was for my daughter Beauty. I promised to bring her back a rose from my journey!" The Beast dropped the paw it had clamped on the unhappy merchant.

"I shall spare your life, but on one condition, that you bring me your daughter!" The terror-stricken merchant, faced with certain death if he did not obey, promised that he would do so. When he reached home in tears, his three daughters ran to greet him. After he had told them of his dreadful adventure, Beauty put his mind at rest immediately.

"Dear father, I'd do anything for you! Don't worry, you'll be able to keep your promise and save your life! Take me to the castle. I'll stay there in your place!" The merchant hugged his daughter.

"I never did doubt your love for me. For the moment I can only thank you for saving my life." So Beauty was led to the castle. The Beast, however, had quite an unexpected greeting for the girl. Instead of menacing doom as it had done with her father, it was surprisingly pleasant.

In the beginning, Beauty was frightened of the Beast, and shuddered at the sight of it. Then she found that, in spite of the monster's awful head, her horror of it was gradually fading as time went by. She had one of the finest rooms in the Castle, and sat for hours, embroidering in front of the fire. And the Beast would sit, for hours on end, only a short distance away, silently gazing at her.

Then it started to say a few kind words, till in the end, Beauty was amazed to discover that she was actually enjoying its conversation. The days passed, and Beauty and the Beast became good friends. Then one day, the Beast asked the girl to be his wife.

Taken by surprise, Beauty did not know what to say. Marry such an ugly monster? She would rather die! But she did not want to hurt the feelings of one who, after all, had been kind to her. And she remembered too that she owed it her own life as well as her father's.

"I really can't say yes," she began shakily. "I'd so much like to . . ." The Beast interrupted her with an abrupt gesture.

"I quite understand! And I'm not offended by your refusal!" Life went on as usual, and nothing further was said. One day, the Beast presented Beauty with a magnificent magic mirror. When Beauty peeped into it, she could see her family, far away.

"You won't feel so lonely now," were the words that accompanied the gift. Beauty stared for hours at her distant family. Then she began to feel worried. One day, the Beast found her weeping beside the magic mirror.

"What's wrong?" he asked, kindly as always.

"My father is gravely ill and close to dying! Oh, how I wish I could see him again, before it's too late!" But the Beast only shook its head.

"No! You will never leave this castle!" And off it stalked in a rage. However, a little later, it returned and spoke solemnly to the girl.

"If you swear that you will return here in seven days time, I'll let you go and visit your father!" Beauty threw herself at the Beast's feet in delight.

"I swear! I swear I will! How kind you are! You've made a loving daughter so happy!" In reality, the merchant had fallen ill from a broken heart at knowing his daughter was being kept prisoner. When he embraced her again, he was soon on the road to recovery. Beauty stayed beside him for hours on end, describing her life at the Castle, and explaining that the Beast was really good and kind. The days flashed past, and at last the merchant was able to leave his bed. He was completely well again. Beauty was happy at last. However, she had failed to notice that seven days had gone by.

Then one night she woke from a terrible nightmare. She had dreamt that the Beast was dying and calling for her, twisting in agony.

"Come back! Come back to me!" it was pleading. The solemn promise she had made drove her to leave home immediately.

"Hurry! Hurry, good horse!" she said, whipping her steed onwards towards the castle, afraid that she might arrive too late. She rushed up the stairs, calling, but there was no reply. Her heart in her mouth, Beauty ran into the garden and there crouched the Beast, its eyes shut, as though dead. Beauty threw herself at it and hugged it tightly.

"Don't die! Don't die! I'll marry you . . ." At these words, a miracle took place. The Beast's ugly snout turned magically into the face of a handsome young man.

"How I've been longing for this moment!" he said. "I was suffering in silence, and couldn't tell my frightful secret. An evil witch turned me into a monster and only the love of a maiden willing to accept me as I was, could transform me back into my real self. My dearest! I'll be so happy if you'll marry me . . ."

The wedding took place shortly after and, from that day on, the young Prince would have nothing but roses in his gardens. And that's why, to this day, the castle is known as the Castle of the Rose.

THE LITTLE GOLD FISH

Once upon a time . . . a poor fisherman lived in a humble cottage near the sea. One day, he set off as usual with his load of nets to go fishing.

"Don't you dare come home empty-handed!" shouted his nagging wife from the door. Down on the shore, he had just thrown the nets into the sea, when something glittering in the meshes caught his eye.

"What a strange fish!" he said to himself, picking up a golden-yellow fish. And his amazement grew when he heard the fish say these words:

"Kind fisherman, let me go free! I'm the son of the Sea King, and if you let me go, I'll grant any wish you care to make!" Alarmed at this miracle, without a second thought, the fisherman tossed the fish back into the water. But when he went home and told his wife what had happened she scolded him soundly:

"What! When the fish said your wishes could come true, you should have asked it for something! Go back to the beach and if you see it, ask for a new washtub! Just look at the state of ours!"

The poor man went back to the shore. As soon as he called the fish, it popped up from the water.

"Were you calling me? Here I am!" it said. The fisherman explained what his wife wanted, and the fish quickly replied:

"You were very good to me! Go home, and you'll see that your wish has come true!" Certain that his wife would be pleased, the fisherman hurried home. But the minute he opened the door, his wife screeched:

"So it really is a magic fish that you allowed to go free! Just look at that old washtub! It's brand new! But if that little fish has such powers, you can't possibly be content with such a miserable little wish! Go straight back and get it to give you a new house!"

The fisherman hurried back to the shore.

"I wonder if I'll see it again! I hope it hasn't gone away! Little fish! Little fish!" he began to call from the water's edge.

"Here I am! What do you want this time?" he heard it ask.

"Well, my wife would like . . ."

"I can imagine!" remarked the fish. "And what does she want now?"

"A big house!" murmured the fisherman, hesitantly.

"All right! You were kind to me and you shall have your wish!" The fisherman lingered on the way home, enjoying the feeling of making his wife happy with a new house. The roof of the splendid new house was already in sight, when his wife rushed

up to him in a fury.

"Look here! Now that we know how really powerful this fish is, we can't be content with only a house! We must ask for more! Run back and ask for a real palace, not an ordinary house like this one! And fine clothes! And jewels too!" The fisherman was quite upset. However, he had been henpecked for so many years that he was unable to say "no",

so he trudged back to the water's edge. Full of doubts, he called the little fish, but it was some time before it leapt from the waves. In the meantime, the sea had begun to foam . . .

"I'm sorry to trouble you again, but my wife has had second thoughts, and she'd like a fine palace, and . . . and also . . ." Again the little fish granted the fisherman his wishes, but he

seemed less friendly than before. At last, relieved at having been able to see his wife's desires fulfilled, the good fisherman turned homewards. Home was now a magnificent palace. How wonderful it was! At the top of a flight of steps leading to the palace, stood his wife, dressed like a great lady and dripping with jewels, impatiently waiting for him.

"Go back and ask for . . ." But the fisherman broke in:

"What? Such a fine palace! We must be content with what we have! Don't you think that's asking too much? . . ."

"Go back, I said! Do as you're told! And ask the fish to make me an Empress!" The poor fisherman set off unhappily for the seashore. In the meantime, a storm had blown up. The sky was black and terrible flashes of lightning lit the darkness, while the waves crashed angrily on the beach. Kneeling on the rock amidst the spray, in a low voice the fisherman began to call the little fish. And when it came, he told it his wife's latest request. But this time, after listening in silence, the little gold fish disappeared beneath the waves without saying a word. And though the fisherman waited, the little fish never came back. A great flash of lightning, much brighter than all the others lit up the sky, and the fisherman saw that both the new house and the palace had vanished without trace. The humble old cottage stood where it had always been. But this time, his wife was waiting for him in tears.

"It serves you right! We should have been pleased with what we had, instead of always asking for more!" grumbled the fisherman angrily. But in the depths of his heart, he was glad that everything had gone back to normal.

Next day and every day, he went back to his fishing, but he never saw the little goldfish again.

THE PRINCESS AND THE PEA

Once upon a time . . . there was a prince who, after wandering the land searching for a wife, returned to his castle and told his unhappy parents that he had been unable to find a bride.

Now, this young man was difficult to please, and he had not been greatly taken with any of the noble young ladies he had met on his travels. He was looking for a bride who was not only beautiful, but also well-born, with the elegance and manners found only in those of noble birth and background.

One evening, during a fierce hurricane that had suddenly blown up, a persistent knocking was heard at the castle door. The prince's father sent a servant to find out who was there. Standing on the steps, lit by flashes of lightning, in the driving rain, was a young lady. "I'm a princess," she said, "seeking shelter for myself and my page. My carriage has broken down and the coachman can't repair it till tomorrow."

In the meantime, the prince's mother had appeared to welcome the guest. She stared disapprovingly at the girl's muddy wet garments, and decided to find out if she really was of gentle birth.

"Prepare a soft soft bed in the Blue Room," she said, "I'll come myself and make sure everything is in order." She told the servants to lay a pile of soft quilts on top of the mattress, and under the mattress she hid a pea. Then she showed the girl to her room. The rain beat down all night and lightning streaked the sky. In the morning, the prince's mother asked her guest: "Did you sleep well? Was the bed comfortable?" The girl politely replied:

"It was a lovely soft bed, so soft that I could feel something hard under the mattress. This morning, I discovered it was a pea. It kept me awake all night!" The prince's mother offered her apologies, before rushing off to her son.

"A real princess at last! Just think! She could feel the pea I hid under the mattress! Now, only a well-born lady could do that!"

The prince had finally found the bride of his dreams. After the wedding, the pea was placed inside a gold and crystal box and exhibited in the castle museum.

HANSEL AND GRETEL

Once upon a time . . . a very poor woodcutter lived in a tiny cottage in the forest with his two children, Hansel and Gretel. His second wife often ill-treated the children and was forever nagging the woodcutter.

"There is not enough food in the house for us all. There are too many mouths to feed! We must get rid of the two brats," she declared. And she kept on trying to persuade her husband to abandon his children in the forest.

"Take them miles from home, so far that they can never find their way back! Maybe someone will find them and give them a home." The downcast woodcutter didn't know what to do. Hansel who, one evening, had overheard his parents' conversation, comforted Gretel.

"Don't worry! If they do leave us in the forest, we'll find the way home," he said. And slipping out of the house he filled his pockets with little white pebbles, then went back to bed.

All night long, the woodcutter's wife harped on and on at her husband till, at dawn, he led Hansel and Gretel away into the forest. But as they went into the depths of the trees, Hansel dropped a little white pebble here and there on the mossy green ground. At a certain point, the two children found they really were alone: the woodcutter had plucked up enough courage to desert them, had mumbled an excuse and was gone.

Night fell but the woodcutter did not return. Gretel began to sob bitterly. Hansel too felt scared but he tried to hide his feelings and comfort his sister.

"Don't cry, trust me! I swear
I'll take you home, even if
Father doesn't come back for
us!" Luckily the moon was full
that night and Hansel waited
till its cold light filtered through
the trees.

"Now give me your hand!"
he said. "We'll get home safely, you'll see!" The tiny white
pebbles gleamed in the moonlight, and the children found their
way home. They crept through a half-open window, without
wakening their parents. Cold, tired but thankful to be home
again, they slipped into bed.

Next day, when their stepmother discovered that Hansel and
Gretel had returned, she went into a rage. Stifling her anger in
front of the children, she locked her bedroom door, reproaching
her husband for failing to carry out her orders. The weak
woodcutter protested, torn as he was between shame and fear of
disobeying his cruel wife. The wicked stepmother kept Hansel
and Gretel under lock and key all day with nothing for supper but
a sip of water and some hard bread. All night, husband and wife
quarrelled, and when dawn came, the woodcutter led the
children out into the forest.

Hansel, however, had not eaten his bread, and as he walked through the trees, he left a trail of crumbs behind him to mark the way. But the little boy had forgotten about the hungry birds that lived in the forest. When they saw him, they flew along behind and in no time at all, had eaten all the crumbs. Again, with a lame excuse, the woodcutter left his two children by themselves.

"I've left a trail, like last time!" Hansel whispered to Gretel, consolingly. But when night fell, they saw to their horror, that all the crumbs had gone.

"I'm frightened!" wept Gretel bitterly. "I'm cold and hungry and I want to go home!"

"Don't be afraid. I'm here to look after you!" Hansel tried to encourage his sister, but he too shivered when he glimpsed frightening shadows and evil eyes around them in the darkness. All night the two children huddled together for warmth at the foot of a large tree.

When dawn broke, they started to wander about the forest, seeking a path, but all hope soon faded. They were well and truly lost. On they walked and walked, till suddenly they came upon a strange cottage in the middle of a glade.

"This is chocolate!" gasped Hansel as he broke a lump of plaster from the wall.

"And this is icing!" exclaimed Gretel, putting another piece of wall in her mouth. Starving but delighted, the children began to eat pieces of candy broken off the cottage.

"Isn't this delicious?" said Gretel, with her mouth full. She had never tasted anything so nice.

"We'll stay here," Hansel declared, munching a bit of nougat. They were just about to try a piece of the biscuit door when it quietly swung open.

"Well, well!" said an old woman, peering out with a crafty look. "And haven't you children a sweet tooth?"

"Come in! Come in, you've nothing to fear!" went on the old woman. Unluckily for Hansel and Gretel, however, the sugar candy cottage belonged to an old witch, her trap for catching unwary victims. The two children had come to a really nasty place . . .

"You're nothing but skin and bones!" said the witch, locking Hansel into a cage. "I shall fatten you up and eat you!"

"You can do the housework," she told Gretel grimly, "then I'll make a meal of you too!" As luck would have it, the witch had very bad eyesight, and when Gretel smeared butter on her glasses, she could see even less.

"Let me feel your finger!" said the witch to Hansel every day, to check if he was getting any fatter. Now, Gretel had brought her brother a chicken bone, and when the witch went to touch his finger, Hansel held out the bone.

"You're still much too thin!" she complained. "When will you become plump?" One day the witch grew tired of waiting.

"Light the oven," she told Gretel. "We're going to have a tasty roasted boy today!" A little later, hungry and impatient, she went on: "Run and see if the oven is hot enough." Gretel returned, whimpering: "I can't tell if it is hot enough or not." Angrily, the witch screamed at the little girl: "Useless child! All right, I'll see for myself." But when the witch bent down to peer inside the oven and check the heat, Gretel gave her a tremendous push and slammed the oven door shut. The witch had come to a fit and proper end. Gretel ran to set her brother free and they made quite sure that the oven door was tightly shut behind the witch. Indeed, just to be on the safe side, they fastened it firmly with a large padlock. Then they stayed for several days to eat some more of the house, till they discovered amongst the witch's belongings, a huge chocolate egg. Inside lay a casket of gold coins.

"The witch is now burnt to a cinder," said Hansel, "so we'll take this treasure with us." They filled a large basket with food and set off into the forest to search for the way home. This time, luck was with them, and on the second day, they saw their father come out of the house towards them, weeping.

"Your stepmother is dead. Come home with me now, my dear children!" The two children hugged the woodcutter.

"Promise you'll never ever desert us again," said Gretel, throwing her arms round her father's neck. Hansel opened the casket.

"Look, Father! We're rich now . . . You'll never have to chop wood again . . ."

And they all lived happily together ever after.

THE WISE LITTLE GIRL

Once upon a time . . . in the immense Russian steppe, lay a little village where nearly all the inhabitants bred horses. It was the month of October, when a big livestock market was held yearly in the main town. Two brothers, one rich and the other one poor, set off for market. The rich man rode a stallion, and the poor brother a young mare.

At dusk, they stopped beside an empty hut and tethered their horses outside, before going to sleep themselves on two heaps of straw. Great was their surprise, when, next morning they saw *three* horses outside, instead of two. Well, to be exact the newcomer was not really a *horse*. It was a foal, to which the mare had given birth during the night. Soon it had the strength to struggle to its feet, and after a drink of its mother's milk, the foal staggered its first few steps. The stallion greeted it with a cheerful whinny, and when the two brothers set eyes on it for the first time, the foal was standing beside the stallion.

"It belongs to me!" exclaimed Dimitri, the rich brother, the minute he saw it. "It's my stallion's foal." Ivan, the poor brother, began to laugh.

"Whoever heard of a stallion having a foal? It was born to my mare!"

"No, that's not true! It was standing close to the stallion, so it's the stallion's foal. And therefore it's mine!" The brothers started to quarrel,

then they decided to go to town and bring the matter before the judges. Still arguing, they headed for the big square where the courtroom stood. But what they didn't know was that it was a special day, the day when, once a year, the Emperor himself administered the law. He himself received all who came seeking justice. The brothers were ushered into his presence, and they told him all about the dispute.

Of course, the Emperor knew perfectly well who was the owner of the foal. He was on the point of proclaiming in favour of the poor brother, when suddenly Ivan developed an unfortunate twitch in his eye. The Emperor was greatly annoyed by this familiarity by a humble peasant, and decided to punish Ivan for his disrespect. After listening to both sides of the story, he declared it was difficult, indeed impossible, to say exactly who was the foal's rightful owner. And being in the mood for a spot of fun, and since he loved posing riddles and solving them as well, to the amusement of his counsellors, he exclaimed:

"I can't judge which of you should have the foal, so it will be awarded to whichever of you solves the following four riddles: what is the fastest thing in the world? What is the fattest? What's the softest and what is the most precious? I command you to return to the palace in a week's time with

37

your answers!" Dimitri started to puzzle over the answers as soon as he left the courtroom. When he reached home, however, he realised he had nobody to help him.

"Well, I'll just have to seek help, for if I can't solve these riddles, I'll lose the foal!" Then he remembered a woman, one of his neighbours, to whom he had once lent a silver ducat. That had been some time ago, and with the interest, the neighbour now owed him *three* ducats. And since she had a reputation for being quick-witted, but also very astute, he decided to ask her advice, in exchange for cancelling part of her debt. But the woman was not slow to show how astute she really was, and promptly demanded that the whole debt be wiped out in exchange for the answers.

"The fastest thing in the world is my husband's bay horse," she said. "Nothing can beat it! The fattest is our pig! Such a huge beast has never been seen! The softest is the quilt I made for the bed, using my own goose's feathers. It's the envy of all my friends. The most precious thing in the world is my three-month old nephew. There isn't a more handsome child. I wouldn't exchange him for all the gold on earth, and that makes him the most precious thing on earth!"

Dimitri was rather doubtful about the woman's answers being correct. On the other hand, he had to take some kind of solution back to the Emperor. And he guessed, quite rightly, that if he didn't, he would be punished.

In the meantime, Ivan, who was a widower, had gone back to the humble cottage where he lived with his small daughter. Only seven years old, the little girl was often left alone, and as a result, was thoughtful and very clever for her age. The poor man took the little girl into his confidence, for like his brother, he knew he would never be able to find the answers by himself. The child sat in silence for a moment, then firmly said:

"Tell the Emperor that the fastest thing in the world is the cold north wind in winter. The fattest is the soil in our fields whose crops give life to men and animals alike, the softest thing is a child's caress and the most precious is honesty."

The day came when the two brothers were to return before the Emperor. They were led into his presence. The Emperor was curious to hear what they had to say, but he roared with laughter at Dimitri's foolish answers. However, when it was Ivan's turn to speak, a frown spread over the Emperor's face. The poor brother's wise replies made him squirm, especially the last one, about honesty, the most precious thing of all. The Emperor knew perfectly well that he had been dishonest in his dealings with the poor brother, for he had denied him justice. But he could not bear to admit it in front of his own counsellors, so he angrily demanded:

"Who gave you these answers?" Ivan told the Emperor that it was his small daughter. Still annoyed, the great man said:

"You shall be rewarded for having such a wise and clever daughter. You shall be awarded the foal that your brother claimed, together with a hundred silver ducats . . . But . . . but . . ." and the Emperor winked at his counsellors:

"You will come before me in seven days' time, bringing your daughter. And since she's so clever, she must appear before me neither naked nor dressed, neither on foot nor on horseback, neither bearing gifts nor empty-handed. And if she does this, you will have your reward. If not, you'll have your head chopped off for your impudence!"

The onlookers began to laugh, knowing that the poor man would never to able to fulfill the Emperor's conditions. Ivan went home in despair, his eyes brimming with tears. But when he had told his daughter what had happened, she calmly said:

"Tomorrow, go and catch a hare and a partridge. Both must be alive! You'll have the foal and the hundred silver ducats! Leave it to me!" Ivan did as his daughter said. He had no idea what the two creatures were for, but he trusted in his daughter's wisdom.

On the day of the audience with the Emperor, the palace was thronged with bystanders, waiting for Ivan and his small daughter to arrive. At last, the little girl appeared, draped in a fishing net, riding the hare and holding the partridge in her hand. She was neither naked nor dressed, on foot or on horseback. Scowling, the Emperor told her:

"I said neither bearing gifts nor empty-handed!" At these words, the little girl held out the partridge. The Emperor stretched out his hand to

grasp it, but the bird fluttered into the air. The third condition had been fulfilled. In spite of himself, the Emperor could not help admiring the little girl who had so cleverly passed such a test, and in a gentler voice, he said:

"Is your father terribly poor, and does he desperately need the foal?"

"Oh, yes!" replied the little girl. "We live on the hares he catches in the rivers and the fish he picks from the trees!"

"Aha!" cried the Emperor triumphantly. "So you're not as clever as you seem to be! Whoever heard of hares in the river and fish in the trees!" To which the little girl swiftly replied:

"And whoever heard of a stallion having a foal?" At that, both Emperor and Court burst into peals of laughter. Ivan was immediately given his hundred silver ducats and the foal, and the Emperor proclaimed:

"Only in *my* kingdom could such a wise little girl be born!"

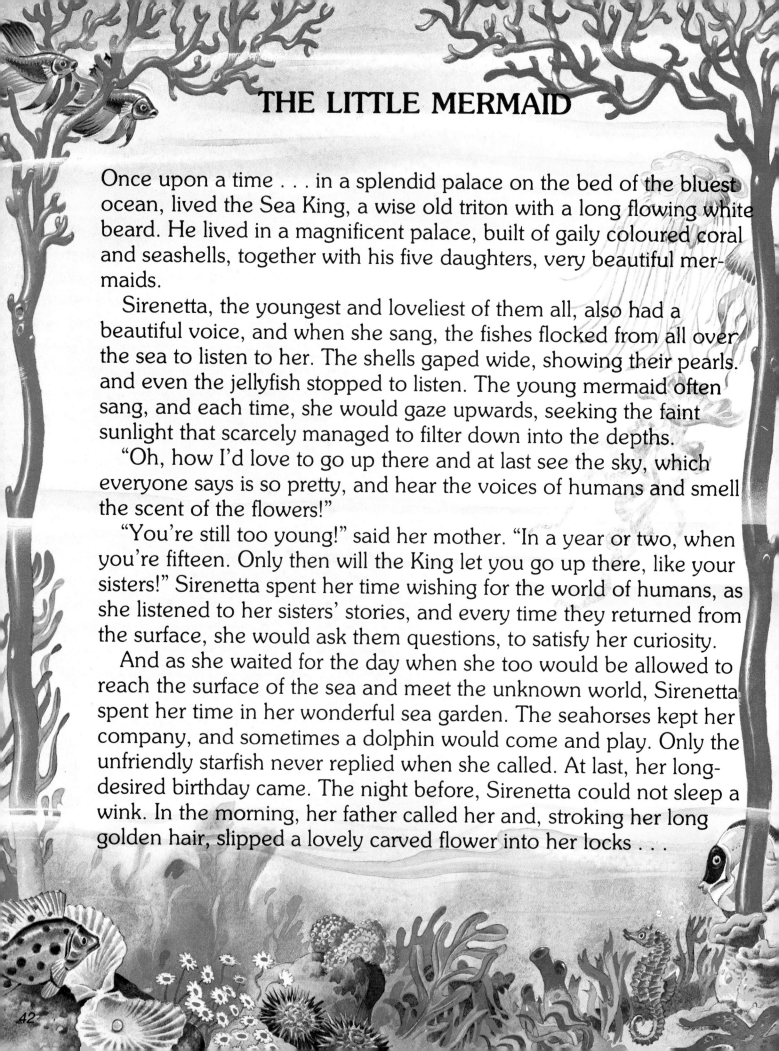

THE LITTLE MERMAID

Once upon a time . . . in a splendid palace on the bed of the bluest ocean, lived the Sea King, a wise old triton with a long flowing white beard. He lived in a magnificent palace, built of gaily coloured coral and seashells, together with his five daughters, very beautiful mermaids.

Sirenetta, the youngest and loveliest of them all, also had a beautiful voice, and when she sang, the fishes flocked from all over the sea to listen to her. The shells gaped wide, showing their pearls. and even the jellyfish stopped to listen. The young mermaid often sang, and each time, she would gaze upwards, seeking the faint sunlight that scarcely managed to filter down into the depths.

"Oh, how I'd love to go up there and at last see the sky, which everyone says is so pretty, and hear the voices of humans and smell the scent of the flowers!"

"You're still too young!" said her mother. "In a year or two, when you're fifteen. Only then will the King let you go up there, like your sisters!" Sirenetta spent her time wishing for the world of humans, as she listened to her sisters' stories, and every time they returned from the surface, she would ask them questions, to satisfy her curiosity.

And as she waited for the day when she too would be allowed to reach the surface of the sea and meet the unknown world, Sirenetta spent her time in her wonderful sea garden. The seahorses kept her company, and sometimes a dolphin would come and play. Only the unfriendly starfish never replied when she called. At last, her long-desired birthday came. The night before, Sirenetta could not sleep a wink. In the morning, her father called her and, stroking her long golden hair, slipped a lovely carved flower into her locks . . .

"There! Now you can go to the surface. You'll breathe air and see the sky. But remember! It's not our world! We can only watch it and admire! We're children of the sea and have no soul, as men do. Be careful and keep away from them; they can only bring bad luck!" In a second, Sirenetta had kissed her father and was darting smoothly towards the surface of the sea. She swam so fast with flicks of her slender tail, that even the fish could not keep up with her.

Suddenly she popped out of the water. How wonderful! For the first time, she saw the great blue sky, in which as dusk began to fall, the first stars were peeping out and twinkling. The sun, already over the horizon, trailed a golden reflection that gently faded on the heaving waves. High overhead, a flock of gulls spotted the little mermaid and greeted her arrival with shrieks of pleasure.

"It's so lovely!" she exclaimed happily. But another nice surprise was in store for her: a ship was slowly sailing towards the rock on which Sirenetta was sitting. The sailors dropped anchor and the ship swayed gently in the calm sea. Sirenetta watched the men go about their work aboard, lighting the lanterns for the night. She could clearly hear their voices.

"I'd love to speak to them!" she said to herself. But then she gazed sadly at her long flexible tail, her equivalent of legs, and said to herself: "I can never be like them!" Aboard ship, a strange excitement seemed to seize the crew, and a little later, the sky became a spray of many coloured lights and the crackle of fireworks filled the sky.

"Long live the captain! Hurray for his 20th birthday. Hurray! Hurray . . . many happy returns!" Astonished at all this, the little mermaid caught sight of the young man in whose honour the display was being held. Tall and dignified, he was smiling happily, and Sirenetta could not take her eyes from him. She followed his every movement, fascinated by all that was happening. The party went on, but the sea grew more agitated. Sirenetta anxiously realized that the men were now in danger: an icy wind was sweeping the waves, the ink black sky was torn by flashes of lightning, then a terrible storm broke suddenly over the helpless ship. In vain Sirenetta screamed: "Look out! Beware of the sea . . ." But the howling wind carried her words away, and the rising waves swept over the ship. Amidst the sailors' shouts, masts and sails toppled onto the deck, and with a sinister splintering sound, the ship sank.

By the light of one of the lamps, Sirenetta had seen the young captain fall into the water, and she swam to his rescue. But she could not find him in the high waves and, tired out, was about to give up, when suddenly there he was on the crest of a nearby wave. In an instant, he was swept straight into the mermaid's arms.

The young man was unconscious and the mermaid held his head above water in the stormy sea, in an effort to save his life. She clung to him for hours trying to fight the tiredness that was overtaking her.

Then, as suddenly as it had sprung up, the storm died away. In a grey dawn over a still angry sea, Sirenetta realized thankfully that land lay ahead. Aided by the motion of the waves, she pushed the captain's body onto the shore, beyond the water's edge. Unable herself to walk, the mermaid sat wringing her hands, her tail lapped by the rippling water, trying to warm the young captain with her own body. Then the sound of approaching voices startled Sirenetta and she slipped back into deeper water.

"Come quickly! Quickly!" came a woman's voice in alarm. "There's a man here! Look, I think he's unconscious!" The captain was now in good hands.

"Let's take him up to the castle!"

"No, no! Better get help . . ." And the first thing the young man saw when he opened his eyes again was the beautiful face of the youngest of a group of three ladies.

"Thank you! Thank you . . . for saving my life . . ." he murmured to the lovely unknown lady.

45

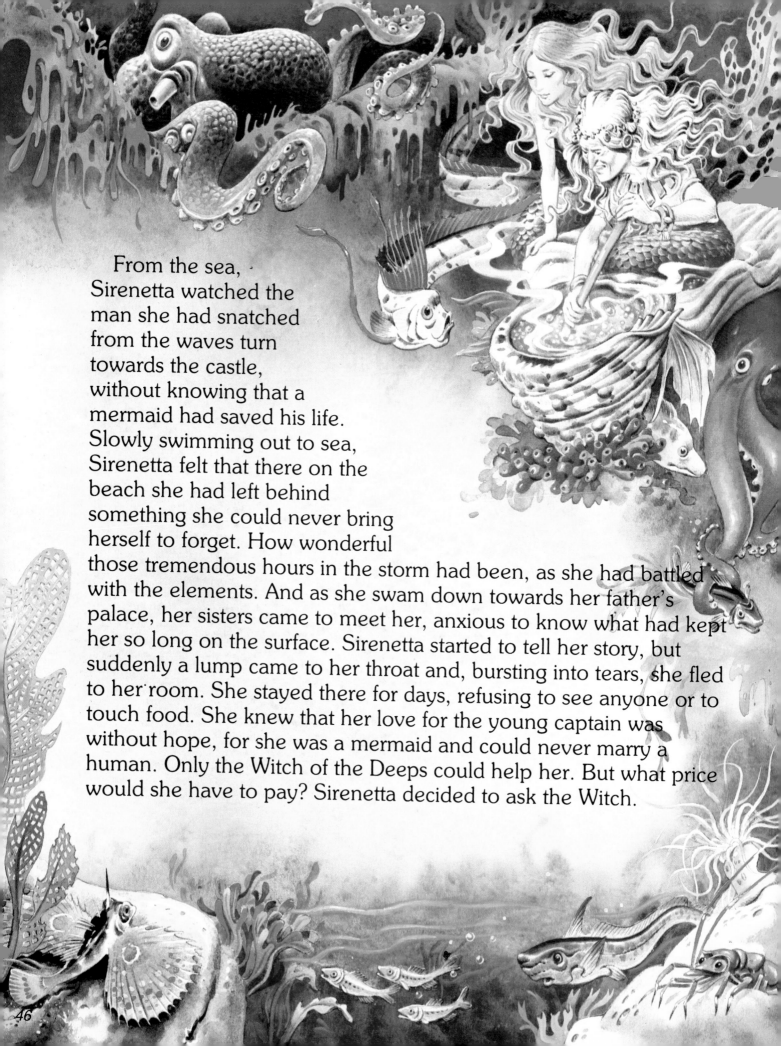

From the sea, Sirenetta watched the man she had snatched from the waves turn towards the castle, without knowing that a mermaid had saved his life. Slowly swimming out to sea, Sirenetta felt that there on the beach she had left behind something she could never bring herself to forget. How wonderful those tremendous hours in the storm had been, as she had battled with the elements. And as she swam down towards her father's palace, her sisters came to meet her, anxious to know what had kept her so long on the surface. Sirenetta started to tell her story, but suddenly a lump came to her throat and, bursting into tears, she fled to her room. She stayed there for days, refusing to see anyone or to touch food. She knew that her love for the young captain was without hope, for she was a mermaid and could never marry a human. Only the Witch of the Deeps could help her. But what price would she have to pay? Sirenetta decided to ask the Witch.

". . . so you want to get rid of your fishy tail, do you? I expect you'd like to have a pair of woman's legs, isn't that so?" said the nasty Witch scornfully, from her cave guarded by a giant squid.

"Be warned!" she went on. "You will suffer horribly, as though a sword were cutting you apart. And every time you place your feet on the earth, you will feel dreadful pain!"

"It doesn't matter!" whispered Sirenetta, with tears in her eyes. "As long as I can go back to him!"

"And that's not all!" exclaimed the Witch. "In exchange for my spell, you must give me your lovely voice. You'll never be able to utter a word again! And don't forget! If the man you love marries someone else, you will not be able to turn into a mermaid again. You will just dissolve in water like the foam on the wave!"

"All right!" said Sirenetta, eagerly taking the little jar holding the magic potion. The Witch had told Sirenetta that the young captain was actually a prince, and the mermaid left the water at a spot not far from the castle. She pulled herself onto the beach, then drank the magic potion. An agonizing pain made her faint, and when she came to her senses, she could mistily see the face she loved, smiling down at her.

The witch's magic had worked the spell, for the prince had felt a strange desire to go down to the beach, just as Sirenetta was arriving. There he had stumbled on her, and recalling how he too had once been washed up on the shore, gently laid his cloak over the still body, cast up by the waves.

"Don't be frightened!" he said quickly. "You're quite safe! Where have you come from?" But Sirenetta was now dumb and could not reply, so the young man softly stroked her wet cheek.

"I'll take you to the castle and look after you," he said. In the days that followed, the

mermaid started a new life. She wore splendid dresses and often went out on horseback with the prince. One evening, she was invited to a great ball at Court. However, as the Witch had foretold, every movement and each step she took was torture. Sirenetta bravely put up with her suffering, glad to be allowed to stay near her beloved prince. And though she could not speak to him, he was fond of her and showered kindness on her, to her great joy. However, the young man's heart really belonged to the unknown lady he had seen as he lay on the shore, though he had never met her since, for she had returned at once to her own land.

Even when he was in the company of Sirenetta, fond of her as he was, the unknown lady was always in his thoughts. And the little mermaid, guessing instinctively that she was not his true love, suffered even more.

She often crept out of the castle at night, to weep by the seashore. Once she thought she could spy her sisters rise from the water and wave at her, but this made her feel sadder than ever.

Fate, however, had another surprise in store. From the Castle ramparts one day, a huge ship was sighted sailing into the harbour. Together with Sirenetta, the prince went down to meet it. And who stepped from the vessel, but the unknown lady who had been for so long in the prince's heart. When he saw her, he rushed to greet her. Sirenetta felt herself turn to stone and a painful feeling pierced her heart: she was about to lose the prince for ever. The unknown lady too had never forgotten the young man she had found on the beach, and soon after, he asked her to marry him. Since she too was in love, she happily said "yes".

A few days after the wedding, the happy couple were invited to go for a voyage on the huge ship, which was still in the harbour. Sirenetta too went on board, and the ship set sail. Night fell, and sick at heart over the loss of the prince, Sirenetta went on deck. She remembered the Witch's prophecy, and was now ready to give up her life and dissolve in the sea. Suddenly she heard a cry from the water and dimly saw her sisters in the darkness.

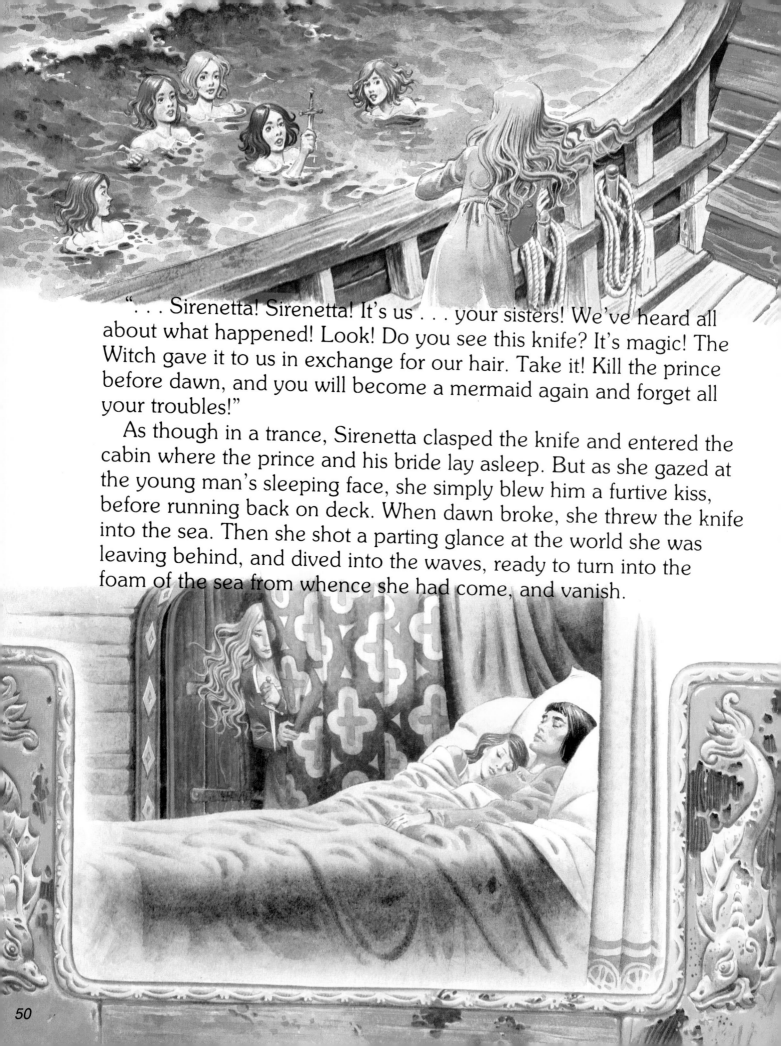

". . . Sirenetta! Sirenetta! It's us . . . your sisters! We've heard all about what happened! Look! Do you see this knife? It's magic! The Witch gave it to us in exchange for our hair. Take it! Kill the prince before dawn, and you will become a mermaid again and forget all your troubles!"

As though in a trance, Sirenetta clasped the knife and entered the cabin where the prince and his bride lay asleep. But as she gazed at the young man's sleeping face, she simply blew him a furtive kiss, before running back on deck. When dawn broke, she threw the knife into the sea. Then she shot a parting glance at the world she was leaving behind, and dived into the waves, ready to turn into the foam of the sea from whence she had come, and vanish.

As the sun rose over the horizon, it cast a long golden ray of light across the sea, and in the chilly water, Sirenetta turned towards it for the last time. Suddenly, as though by magic, a mysterious force drew her out of the water, and she felt herself lifted high into the sky. The clouds were tinged with pink, the sea rippled in the early morning breeze, and the little mermaid heard a whisper through the tinkling of bells: "Sirenetta, Sirenetta! Come with us . . ."

"Who are you?" asked the mermaid, surprised to find she had recovered the use of her voice. "Where am I?"

"You're with us in the sky. We're the fairies of the air! We have no soul as men do, but our task is to help them. We take amongst us only those who have shown kindness to men!"

Greatly touched, Sirenetta looked down over the sea towards the prince's ship, and felt tears spring to her eyes. The fairies of the air whispered to her: "Look! The earth flowers are waiting for our tears to turn into the morning dew! Come along with us . . ."

Once upon a time . . .

. . . a big bad wolf was roaming hungrily through a great forest. One day, he saw a basket covered with a white cloth lying on the ground, and his greedy eyes peered around . . .

LITTLE RED RIDING HOOD

Once upon a time . . . in the middle of a thick forest stood a small cottage, the home of a pretty little girl known to everyone as Little Red Riding Hood. One day, her Mummy waved her goodbye at the garden gate, saying: "Grandma is ill. Take her this basket of cakes, but be very careful. Keep to the path through the wood and don't ever stop. That way, you will come to no harm."

Little Red Riding Hood kissed her mother and ran off. "Don't worry,' she said, "I'll run all the way to Grandma's without stopping."

Full of good intentions, the little girl made her way through the wood, but she was soon to forget her mother's wise words. "What lovely strawberries! And so red . . ."

Laying her basket on the ground, Little Red Riding Hood bent over the strawberry plants. "They're nice and ripe, and so big! Yummy! Delicious! Just another one. And one more. This is the last . . . Well, *this* one . . . Mmmm."

The red fruit peeped invitingly through the leaves in the grassy glade, and Little Red Riding Hood ran back and forth popping strawberries into her mouth. Suddenly she remembered her mother, her promise, Grandma and the basket . . . and hurried back towards the path. The basket was still in the grass and, humming to herself, Little Red Riding Hood walked on.

The wood became thicker and thicker. Suddenly a yellow
butterfly fluttered down through the trees. Little Red Riding
Hood started to chase the butterfly.
"I'll catch you! I'll catch you!" she called. Suddenly she saw
some large daisies in the grass.
"Oh, how sweet!" she exclaimed and, thinking of Grandma,
she picked a large bunch of flowers.
In the meantime, two wicked eyes were spying on her from
behind a tree . . a strange rustling in the woods made Little
Red Riding Hood's heart thump.

Now quite afraid, she said to herself, "I must find the path and run away from here!"

At last, she reached the path again, but her heart leapt into her mouth at the sound of a gruff voice which said: "Where are you going, my pretty girl, all alone in the woods?"

"I'm taking Grandma some cakes. She lives at the end of the path," said Little Riding Hood in a faint voice.

When he heard this, the wolf (for it was the big bad wolf himself) politely asked: "Does Grandma live by herself?"

"Oh, yes," replied Little Red Riding Hood, "and she never opens the door to strangers!"

"Goodbye. Perhaps we'll meet again," replied the wolf. Then he loped away thinking to himself "I'll gobble the grandmother first, then lie in wait for the grandchild!" At last, the cottage came in sight. Knock! Knock! The wolf rapped on the door.

"Who's there?" cried Grandma from her bed.

"It's me, Little Red Riding Hood. I've brought you some cakes because you're ill," replied the wolf, trying hard to hide his gruff voice.

"Lift the latch and come in," said Grandma, unaware of anything amiss, till a horrible shadow appeared on the wall. Poor Grandma! For in one bound, the wolf leapt across the room and, in a single mouthful, swallowed the old lady. Soon after, Little Red Riding Hood tapped on the door.

"Grandma, can I come in?" she called.

Now, the wolf had put on the old lady's shawl and cap and slipped into the bed. Trying to imitate Grandma's quavering little voice, he replied: "Open the latch and come in!"

"What a deep voice you have," said the little girl in surprise.

"The better to greet you with," said the wolf.

"Goodness, what big eyes you have."

"The better to see you with."

"And what big hands you have!" exclaimed Little Red Riding Hood, stepping over to the bed.

"The better to hug you with," said the wolf.

"What a big mouth you have," the little girl murmured in a weak voice.

"The better to eat you with!" growled the wolf, and jumping out of bed, he swallowed her up too. Then, with a fat full tummy, he fell fast asleep.

In the meantime, a hunter had emerged from the wood, and on noticing the cottage, he decided to stop and ask for a drink. He had spent a lot of time trying to catch a large wolf that had been terrorizing the neighbourhood, but had lost its tracks. The hunter could hear a strange whistling sound; it seemed to be coming from inside the cottage. He peered through the window . . . and saw the large wolf himself, with a fat full tummy, snoring away in Grandma's bed.

"The wolf! He won't get away this time!"

Without making a sound, the hunter carefully loaded his gun and gently opened the window. He pointed the barrel straight at the wolf's head and . . . BANG! The wolf was dead.

"Got you at last!" shouted the hunter in glee. "You'll never frighten anyone again."

He cut open the wolf's stomach and to his amazement, out popped Grandma and Little Red Riding Hood, safe and unharmed.

"You arrived just in time," murmured the old lady, quite overcome by all the excitement.

"It's safe to go home now," the hunter told Little Red Riding Hood. "The big bad wolf is dead and gone, and there is no danger on the path."

Still scared, the little girl hugged her grandmother. "Oh, what a dreadful fright!"

Much later, as dusk was falling, Little Red Riding Hood's mother arrived, all out of breath, worried because her little girl had not come home. And when she saw Little Red Riding Hood, safe and sound, she burst into tears of joy.

After thanking the hunter again, Little Red Riding Hood and her mother set off towards the wood. As they walked quickly through the trees, the little girl told her mother: "We must always keep to the path and never stop. That way, we'll come to no harm!"

THE MAGIC TINDERBOX

Once upon a time . . . a brave soldier returned from the wars. In spite of his courage, his pockets were empty and his only possession was his sword. As he walked through a forest, he met a witch, who said to him: "I say, good soldier, would you like to earn a bag of money?"

"Money? I'd do anything for money . . ."

"Good!" went on the witch. "It won't be difficult, you'll see! All you have to do is go down that hollow tree till you reach a cave. There, you'll find three doorways. When you open the first door, you'll see a big dog with eyes like saucers, guarding a large chest of copper coins. Behind the second door lies a treasure of silver coins, guarded by a dog with eyes the size of mill stones. When you open the third door, you'll come upon another dog, with eyes the size of a castle tower, beside a treasure of gold. Now, if you lay this old apron of mine before these dogs, they'll crouch on it and do you no harm. You'll be able to carry away all the coins you want. What do think of that?"

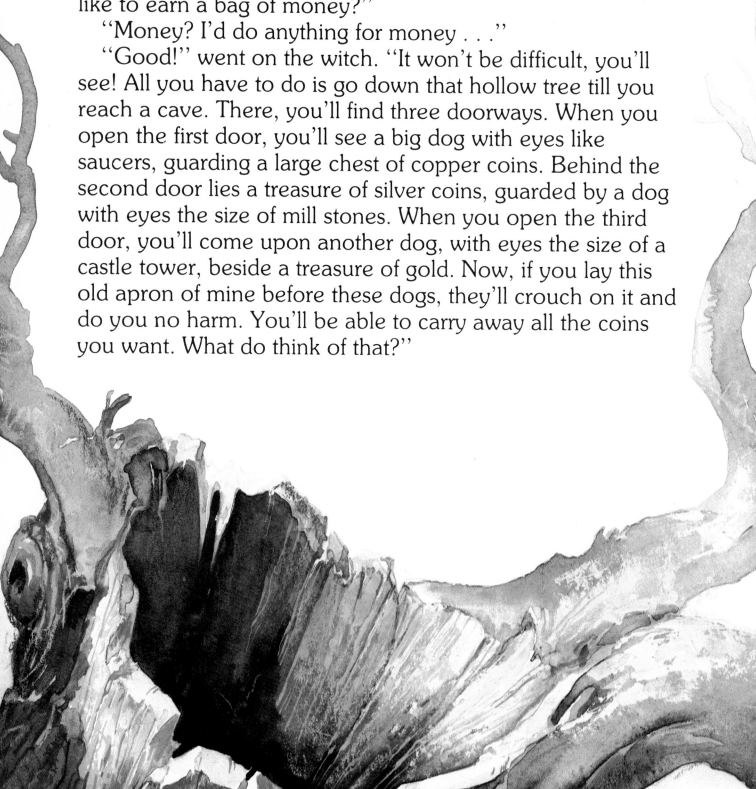

However, the soldier suspiciously asked: "What do you want in return?"

"Just bring me back an old tinderbox my grandfather left down there, long ago!"

So the young soldier tied a rope round his waist and, not forgetting his trusty sword, he lowered himself into the hollow tree. To his great surprise, he found the three doorways and the three dogs, just as the witch had said. Soon he was back, his pockets bulging with coins, but before he handed the tinderbox to the old witch, he asked her: "What do you want it for?"

The witch hurled herself at the soldier, screaming: "Give it to me! Give it to me at once, or else . . .", as she tried to

scratch him. When the witch attacked him, the soldier exclaimed: "Aha! So this is the thanks I get! Now I'll show *you*!"

He undid the rope from around his waist and tied up the old woman. Then away he went, whistling cheerfully.

When he reached the town, he said to himself: "Now I can feast as much as I like – at last!"

After years of scrimping on a miserable pay, with his sudden wealth, the soldier felt like a prince. He bought a new pair of boots and he went to the best tailor in the town. Some days later, he was clad in a fine new uniform and people turned in the street to admire him. Lavish with his money, the soldier was surrounded by folk quick to tell him how to spend his coins, and it all went on a round of dances, fine carriages, theatres and, most of all, on drinking sprees. Of course, his money soon ran out and when this happened, his "friends" vanished. When the innkeeper discovered that the soldier could no longer pay his board, he rudely put him out. So the poor soldier ended up in a garret and every day he had to draw in his belt a little more. All the fun was over.

One evening, he realized he had never used the old witch's tinderbox. So he rubbed it, and as it sparked, the dog with the eyes like saucers suddenly appeared.

"Tell me your wish, sir," it said.

". . . bring me heaps of money!" gasped the soldier in amazement. A second later, the dog was back with a bag of coins. Every time he rubbed the tinderbox, the dog brought him more money. Then when he rubbed it quickly twice in succession, the dog with eyes like mill stones stood before him, carrying silver coins. And when the soldier rubbed the tinderbox three times in a row, the third dog came carrying gold. Rich all over again, the soldier chose the best hotel in the town and went back to leading the life of a fine gentleman.

The soldier was told that the King would not allow anyone

to meet his beautiful daughter, for he believed in a saying that the Princess's destiny was to marry a simple soldier. That evening, the soldier rubbed the tinderbox. "Bring me the Princess," was his new order. Immediately the dog returned with the beautiful Princess, fast asleep. The soldier kissed her. Next morning, the girl told her parents that she had had a dream. But the Queen, suspiciously ordered one of the ladies-in-waiting to guard her daughter day and night. The dog was seen when it came next evening and the alarm raised. The king's guards followed the dog and the soldier was arrested at dawn.

The King's revenge was terrible: the soldier was to be hanged!

In a dark prison, the soldier calmly awaited his fate. When the day of execution came, a mob crushed round the scaffold.

The soldier asked if he could smoke his pipe, and placed it between his lips, as he rubbed the tinderbox over and over again. In a flash, the three dogs appeared with gaping jaws and bloodshot eyes. At the soldier's sharp command, they leapt on the guards and the crowd cheered in delight.

Awestruck at this magic feat, the King bowed his head and whispered to the Queen. "The saying is true!" he said. A little while after, the young soldier married the Princess and the tinderbox was rubbed and rubbed, but this time to invite the three dogs to the splendid wedding.

THE LITTLE MATCHGIRL

Once upon a time . . . a little girl tried to make a living by selling matches in the street.

It was New Year's Eve and the snowclad streets were deserted. From brightly lit windows came the tinkle of laughter and the sound of singing. People were getting ready to bring in the New Year. But the poor little matchseller sat sadly beside the fountain. Her ragged dress and worn shawl did not keep out the cold and she tried to keep her bare feet from touching the frozen ground. She hadn't sold one box of matches all day and she was frightened to go home, for her father would certainly be angry. It wouldn't be much warmer anyway, in the draughty attic that was her home. The little girl's fingers were stiff with cold. If only she could light a match! But what would her father say at such a waste! Falteringly she took out a match and lit it. What a nice warm flame! The little matchseller cupped her hand over it, and as she did so, she magically saw in its light a big brightly burning stove.

She held out her hands to the heat, but just then the match went out and the vision faded. The night seemed blacker than before and it was getting colder. A shiver ran through the little girl's thin body.

After hesitating for a long time, she struck another match on the wall, and this time, the glimmer turned the wall into a great sheet of crystal. Beyond that stood a fine table laden with food and lit by a candlestick. Holding out her arms towards the plates, the little matchseller seemed to pass through the glass, but then the match went out and the magic faded. Poor thing: in just a few seconds she had caught a glimpse of everything that life had denied her: warmth and good things to eat. Her eyes filled with tears and she lifted her gaze to the lit windows, praying that she too might know a little of such happiness.

She lit the third match and an even more wonderful thing
happened. There stood a Christmas tree hung with hundreds of
candles, glittering with tinsel and coloured balls. "Oh, how
lovely!" exclaimed the little matchseller, holding up the match.
Then, the match burned her finger and flickered out. The light
from the Christmas candles rose higher and higher, then one of
the lights fell, leaving a trail behind it. "Someone is dying,"
murmured the little girl, as she remembered her beloved Granny
who used to say: "When a star falls, a heart stops beating!"
   Scarcely aware of what she was doing, the little matchseller lit
another match. This time, she saw her grandmother.

"Granny, stay with me!" she pleaded, as she lit one match after the other, so that her grandmother could not disappear like all the other visions. However, Granny did not vanish, but gazed smilingly at her. Then she opened her arms and the little girl hugged her crying: "Granny, take me away with you!"

A cold day dawned and a pale sun shone on the fountain and the icy road. Close by lay the lifeless body of a little girl surrounded by spent matches.

"Poor little thing!" exclaimed the passersby. "She was trying to keep warm!"

But by that time, the little matchseller was far away where there is neither cold, hunger nor pain.

THE PIED PIPER OF HAMELIN

Once upon a time . . . on the banks of a great river in the north of Germany lay a town called Hamelin. The citizens of Hamelin were honest folk who lived contentedly in their grey stone houses. The years went by, and the town grew very rich. Then one day, an extraordinary thing happened to disturb the peace. Hamelin had always had rats, and a lot too. But they had never been a danger, for the cats had always solved the rat problem in the usual way – by killing them. All at once, however, the rats began to multiply.

In the end, a black sea of rats swarmed over the whole town. First, they attacked the barns and storehouses, then, for lack of anything better, they gnawed the wood, cloth or anything at all. The one thing they didn't eat was metal. The terrified citizens flocked to plead with the town councillors to free them from the plague of rats. But the council had, for a long time, been sitting in the Mayor's room, trying to think of a plan.

"What we need is an army of cats!"
But all the cats were dead.
"We'll put down poisoned food then . . ."

But most of the food was already gone and even poison did not stop the rats.

"It just can't be done without help!" said the Mayor sadly.

Just then, while the citizens milled around outside, there was a loud knock at the door. "Who can that be?" the city fathers wondered uneasily, mindful of the angry crowds. They gingerly opened the door. And to their surprise, there stood a tall thin man dressed in brightly coloured clothes, with a long feather in his hat, and waving a gold pipe at them.

"I've freed other towns of beetles and bats," the stranger announced, "and for a thousand florins, I'll rid you of your rats!"

"A thousand florins!" exclaimed the Mayor. "We'll give you *fifty thousand* if you succeed!" At once the stranger hurried away, saying: "It's late now, but at dawn tomorrow, there won't be a rat left in Hamelin!"

The sun was still below the horizon, when the sound of a pipe wafted through the streets of Hamelin. The pied piper slowly made his way through the houses and behind him flocked the rats. Out they scampered from doors, windows and gutters, rats of every size, all after the piper. And as he played, the stranger marched down to the river and straight into the water, up to his middle. Behind him swarmed the rats and every one was drowned and swept away by the current.

By the time the sun was high in the sky, there was not a single rat in the town. There was even greater delight at the town hall, until the piper tried to claim his payment.

"Fifty thousand florins?" exclaimed the councillors, "Never . . ."

" A thousand florins at least!" cried the pied piper angrily. But the Mayor broke in. "The rats are all dead now and they can never come back. So be grateful for fifty florins, or you'll not get even that . . ."

His eyes flashing with rage, the pied piper pointed a threatening finger at the Mayor.

"You'll bitterly regret ever breaking your promise," he said, and vanished.

A shiver of fear ran through the councillors, but the Mayor shrugged and said excitedly: "We've saved fifty thousand florins!"

That night, freed from the nightmare of the rats, the citizens of Hamelin slept more soundly than ever. And when the strange sound of piping wafted through the streets at dawn, only the children heard it. Drawn as by magic, they hurried out of their homes. Again, the pied piper paced through the town, but this time, it was children of all sizes that flocked at his heels to the sound of his strange piping. The long procession soon left the town and made its way through the wood and across the forest till it reached the foot of a huge mountain. When the piper came to the dark rock, he played his pipe even louder still and a great door creaked open.

Beyond lay a cave. In trooped the children behind the pied piper, and when the last child had gone into the darkness, the door creaked shut. A great landslide came down the mountain blocking the entrance to the cave forever. Only one little lame boy escaped this fate. It was he who told the anxious citizens, searching for their children, what had happened. And no matter what people did, the mountain never gave up its victims. Many years were to pass before the merry voices of other children would ring through the streets of Hamelin but the memory of the harsh lesson lingered in everyone's heart and was passed down from father to son through the centuries.

THE SNOW QUEEN

Once upon a time . . . a magician made a magic mirror. In this mirror, a kind face became wicked, a look of hate was reflected as a look of love. One day, however, the mirror broke, and if a sliver of glass from the mirror entered someone's eye, that person's soul became evil, if another pierced a heart, that heart grew hard and cold as ice.

In a big town, two children, called Karl and Gerda were very close friends, and even the sweet pea that grew on Karl's window sill spread across the street to entwine with Gerda's little rose bush. One evening Karl was watching the snow drift down, when he noticed a white flake slowly turn into a beautiful ice maiden. Karl was startled to hear the ice maiden speak his name, and he was not to know he had set eyes on the Snow Queen. Winter passed, and one spring afternoon, as Karl and Gerda pored over a book, the little boy told her: "I feel a pain in my heart! And something's pricking my eye!"

"Don't worry," said Gerda comfortingly. "I can't see anything!" But, alas, splinters from the shattered mirror had pierced the little boy.

Now in the grip of the evil spell, he snapped: "You're so ugly!" And ripping two roses from her bush, he ran off. From that day on, Karl turned into a very nasty boy, and nobody could understand what had happened to him to cause such a change. Only Gerda still loved him, though all she got in return were insults and spite.

Winter came round again, though earlier than usual, and bringing far more snow than anyone could remember.

One day, just after going outdoors to play in the snow, Karl saw the beautiful maiden he had seen that night, coming towards him wrapped in a white fur coat. She stood in front of him and told him to tie his sledge to her own, drawn by a white horse. Then they sped away. Suddenly, the great sledge soared into the sky and through the clouds. Stretched out on his own little sledge, Karl didn't dare move a muscle for fear of falling into space. At last, they came to a halt on an immense white plain, dotted with lots of sparkling frozen lakes.

"Come into my arms," said the Snow Queen, opening her soft fur coat. "Come and keep warm!"

Karl allowed himself to be hugged by the unknown maiden and a chill ran up his spine as two icy lips touched his forehead. The Snow Queen kissed him again, and in an instant, the little boy forgot all about Gerda and his past life, as he fell into a deep sleep.

In the meantime, Gerda was anxiously searching for Karl, but no one had seen him. Finally, she went down to the river.

"Great river," she said, "please tell me if you've seen Karl or if you've carried him away! I'll give you these, if you do!" And she threw her shoes into the river. But the current paid no heed and just swept them back to the bank. Not far away stood an old boat, and Gerda climbed into it. As she drifted with the current, she pleaded: "Great river, silently flowing and knowing all things about men's lives, take me to Karl."

At dusk, she stopped by a river bank carpeted with all kinds of flowers. After resting she went into the forest, and though she did not know how she would ever find her friend, a mysterious voice inside her told her to be brave. After wandering far and wide, she stopped, tired and hungry. A crow flapped out from a hollow tree.

"If you're looking for Karl," it said, "I know where he is! I saw him with the Snow Queen on her sledge in the sky!"

"And where is her kingdom?" Gerda asked the crow.

"In Lapland, where all is icy cold. That reindeer over there might take you!"

Gerda ran over to the big reindeer, threw her arms around its neck and, laying her cheek against its soft muzzle, said: "Please help me to find my friend!"

The reindeer's kindly eyes told her that he would, and she

climbed onto its back. They travelled till they came to the frozen tundra, lit by the fiery glow of the Northern Lights.

"Karl! Karl! Where are you?" shouted Gerda as loudly as she could. When, at last, she found the little boy, Karl did not recognize her. Gerda threw her arms round him, and teardrops dripped onto his chest and heart. This broke the evil spell. Karl woke from his long sleep, and when he set eyes on Gerda, he too began to cry. The second cold splinter of mirror vanished. They had found each other again at last, thanks to Gerda's love, and the reindeer galloped them home. The two plants on the window sills started to blossom again and to twine, a sign of their everlasting friendship.

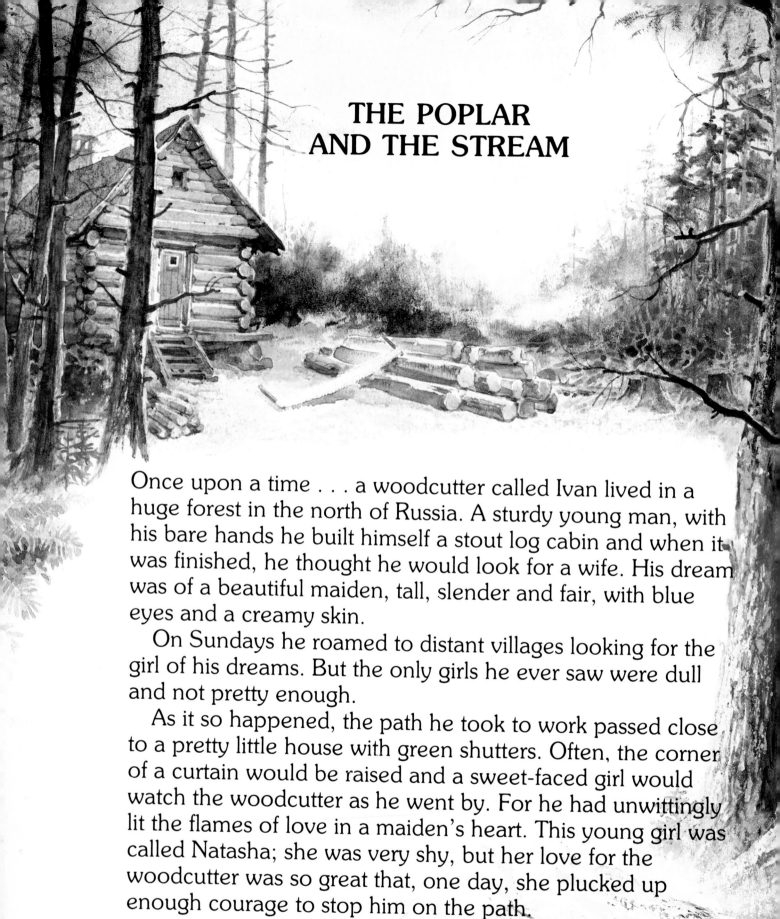

THE POPLAR
AND THE STREAM

Once upon a time . . . a woodcutter called Ivan lived in a huge forest in the north of Russia. A sturdy young man, with his bare hands he built himself a stout log cabin and when it was finished, he thought he would look for a wife. His dream was of a beautiful maiden, tall, slender and fair, with blue eyes and a creamy skin.

On Sundays he roamed to distant villages looking for the girl of his dreams. But the only girls he ever saw were dull and not pretty enough.

As it so happened, the path he took to work passed close to a pretty little house with green shutters. Often, the corner of a curtain would be raised and a sweet-faced girl would watch the woodcutter as he went by. For he had unwittingly lit the flames of love in a maiden's heart. This young girl was called Natasha; she was very shy, but her love for the woodcutter was so great that, one day, she plucked up enough courage to stop him on the path.

"I picked this basket of strawberries myself," she said. "Please eat them and think of me!"

"Well, she's not exactly ugly," said Ivan to himself as he stared woodenly at Natasha, who was blushing to the roots of her hair.

"I don't like strawberries," he replied bluntly. "But thanks all the same!"

Tears sprang to Natasha's eyes as she watched him stride away. A few days later, the girl again stopped Ivan and held out a woollen jacket, saying: "The air will be chilly tonight when you go home. This will keep you warm. I made it myself."

But Ivan coldly replied: "What makes you think that a man like me is afraid of the cold?"

And this time, at Ivan's refusal, two tears rolled down Natasha's rosy cheeks and she fled sobbing into the house.

However, Natasha again watched for the woodcutter. This time, she held out a bottle and said: "You can't refuse a liqueur that I distilled from all the fruits of the forest! It will . . ." But Ivan broke in saying: "I don't like liqueurs," and marched straight on. However, he realized he had been very rude, so he turned round, but Natasha had gone. As he walked, he said to himself: " She has gentle eyes . . . and she must be very kind-hearted! Perhaps I should take at least one of her gifts, but . . ."
The picture of his dream girl slipped into his mind.
"I'm so unhappy!" he sighed.

At that very moment, on a golden cloud appeared a beautiful lady. "Will you sing a song for me? I'm Rosalka, one of the woodland fairies!" Ivan stood thunderstruck.

"I'd sing for you for the rest of my life!" he exclaimed. "If only I could . . ." and he stretched out his hand to touch the fairy, but she floated out of reach amongst the branches.

"Sing then! Sing! Only the sound of your voice will ever send me to sleep!" So Ivan happily sang all the old lullabies and love songs, while the drowsy fairy urged him on: "Sing! Sing!"

Cold and weary, his voice getting hoarser the woodcutter sang till evening, as he tried to help the fairy to fall asleep. But when night fell, Rosalka was still demanding: "If you love me, sing on! Sing!"

As the woodcutter sang on, in a feeble voice, he kept thinking: "I wish I had a jacket to keep me warm!"

Suddenly he remembered Natasha.

"What a fool I am!" he told himself. "I should have chosen her as my bride, not this woman who asks and gives nothing in return!"

Ivan felt that only the gentle-faced Natasha could fill his empty heart. He fled into the darkness, but he heard a cruel voice call: ". . . you'll never see her again! All her tears for her great love have turned her into a stream! You'll never see her again!"

It was dawn when Ivan knocked at Natasha's door. No one answered. And the woodcutter saw, with fear, that close by flowed a tiny sparkling stream he had never noticed before. Weeping sorrowfully, he plunged his face into the water.

"Oh, Natasha, how could I have been so blind! And I love you now!" Lifting his gaze to the sky, he silently said a prayer: "Let me stay beside her forever!"

Ivan was magically turned into a young poplar tree and the stream bathed its roots. Natasha had, at last, her beloved Ivan by her side for ever.

THE LITTLE GOLDEN BIRD

Once upon a time . . . several Buddhist monks lived in a great temple that stood in a magnificent garden full of flowers and rare plants. The monks spent their days contentedly in prayer and meditation, and the beauty of their surroundings was all they needed to make them forget the world. Then one day, something happened to change their life in this peaceful corner, making the days seem shorter and not so monotonous. No longer did they live peacefully together, indeed they started to quarrel. But what had happened?

A young monk had arrived, upsetting their lives by telling them all about the outside world beyond the garden wall. He told them about cities, the bright lights, everyday life full of entertainments and pleasure. And when the monks heard about this different world, they no longer wanted to remain in what had, till then, seemed paradise, but now turned into a lonely existence.

With the young monk as their leader, first one group then another left the temple. Weeds began to sprout on the paths and the temple was almost deserted. Then the last five monks, torn between their love for the sacred spot and the wish to see the new world they'd heard about, sadly got ready to leave.

But just as they were about to turn their backs on the temple, a golden bird, dangling five long white strings, fluttered over their heads. Each monk felt himself drawn to clasp one of the strings, and suddenly the little group found itself carried away to the land of their dreams. And there, they saw the outside world as it really was, full of hate, misery and violence, a world without scruples, where peace was forever banned.

It was a long journey, and when the golden bird brought them back to the temple garden, they decided never to leave it again. Three times the bird circled overhead before it vanished into the sky. And the monks knew then that Buddha had come to help them find the pathway to true happiness.

NARCISSUS

Once upon a time . . . in Ancient Greece lived a young man called Narcissus, who was greatly admired, for he was very handsome. Narcissus was very proud of his perfect face and graceful body, and never lost the chance to look at his reflection in any sheet of water he happened to pass. He would lie for hours admiring his gleaming dark eyes, slender nose, slim hips and the mop of curly hair that crowned the perfect oval of his face. You would think a sculptor had come down from heaven to carve such a faultless body as a living image of mankind's love of beauty.

One day, Narcissus was walking close to a precipice where the clear waters of a cold mountain pool mirrored his beautiful face.

"You *are* handsome, Narcissus!" he told himself as he bent down to admire his reflection. "There's nobody so handsome in the whole world! I'd love to kiss you."

Narcissus was suddenly seized by the desire to kiss his own reflection and he leant closer to the water. But he lost his balance and toppled into the pool. Narcissus could not swim and so he drowned. But when the gods discovered that the most beautiful being on earth had died, they decided that such beauty could not be forgotten.

The gods turned Narcissus into a scented flower which, to this day, blossoms in the mountains in spring, and which is still called Narcissus.

THE RUBY PRINCE

Once upon a time . . . a beggar in faraway Persia had a stroke of luck. After a sudden flood, the fast-flowing river near the capital city shrank back to its old bed, leaving mud and slime behind it on the banks. In the dirt, the beggar caught sight of a sparkling red stone. He picked it up and hurried off to visit one of his friends who worked in the royal kitchens.

"How many dinners would you give me for this shining stone?" he asked the man hopefully.

"But this is a ruby!" exclaimed the cook. "You must take it to the Shah at once!" So next day, the beggar took the stone to the Shah, who asked him: "Where did you find this?"

"Lying in the mud on the bank of the river, Sire!" he said.

"Hmm!" mused the Shah. "Now why did the great river leave such a treasure to *you*? I'll give you a bag of gold for the stone. Will that do?" The beggar could scarcely believe his ears.

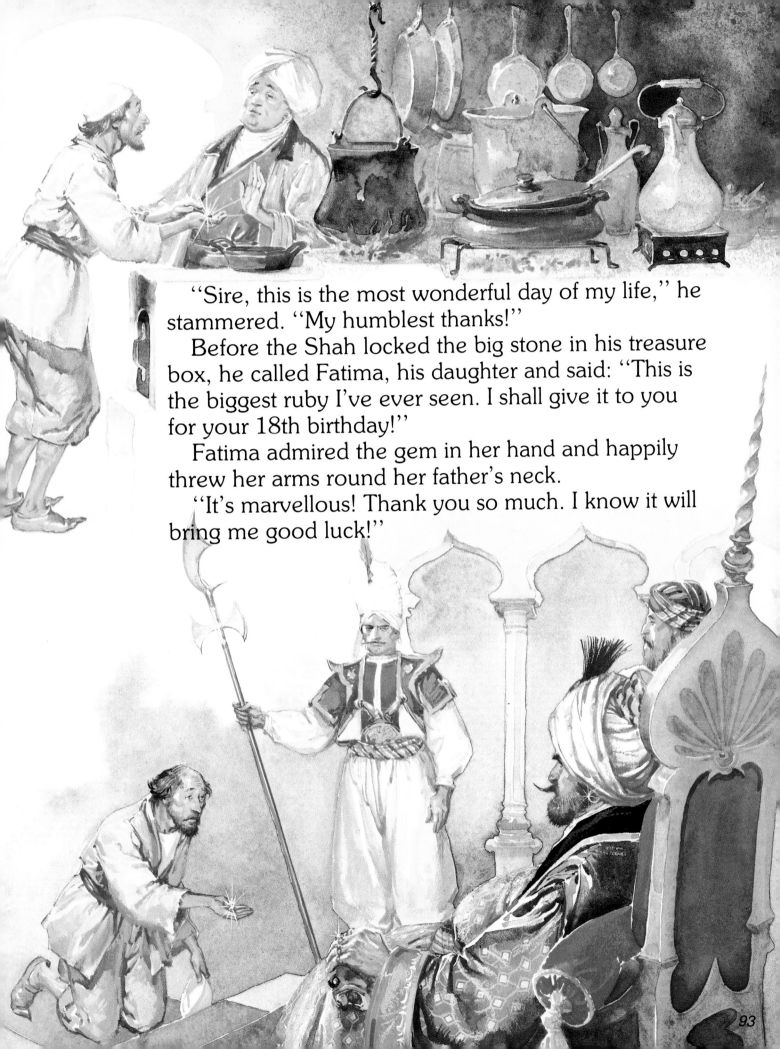

"Sire, this is the most wonderful day of my life," he stammered. "My humblest thanks!"

Before the Shah locked the big stone in his treasure box, he called Fatima, his daughter and said: "This is the biggest ruby I've ever seen. I shall give it to you for your 18th birthday!"

Fatima admired the gem in her hand and happily threw her arms round her father's neck.

"It's marvellous! Thank you so much. I know it will bring me good luck!"

Some months later, on Fatima's birthday, the Shah went to fetch the ruby as promised. But when he lifted the lid of the box, he leapt in surprise, for out stepped a handsome young man, who smilingly said, "The ruby you want no longer exists! I've taken its place. I'm the Ruby Prince. Please don't ask me how this miracle took place. It's a secret I can never tell!"

When the Shah got over his shock, he went into a towering rage. "I lose a precious gem, find a prince, and I'm not allowed to ask the reason why?" he roared.

"I'm sorry, Sire," replied the prince, "but nothing and nobody will make me tell how I got here."

Furious at these words, the Shah instantly decided to punish the young man for his impertinence.

"Since you've taken the place of my ruby," he thundered, "you are now my servant, I presume."

"Of course, Sire," replied the young man confidently.

"Good!" exclaimed the Shah. "Then take my gold sword. I'll reward you with the hand of my daughter Fatima if you succeed in killing the dragon of Death Valley that's stopping the caravans from passing through the forest."

As it happens, many a brave young man had lost his life trying to kill the terrible dragon, and the Shah was quite sure that the Ruby Prince would share their fate.

Armed with the Shah's sword, the Ruby Prince set off for Death Valley. When he reached the edge of the thick dark forest, he loudly called for the dragon to show itself. But the only reply was the echo of his own voice. He leant against a tree trunk and was about to drop off to sleep when the sound of snapping branches brought him to his feet. A frightful hissing grew louder and louder and the earth trembled. The terrible dragon was on its way.

Before him the huge horrible beast reared with open jaws.
Unlike all the other brave warriors who had gone before him, the
prince stoutly stood his ground; he took a step forward and
struck first one heavy blow at the dragon's throat, then another,
till at last the monster lay dead at his feet.

When he returned to the palace carrying the dragon's head,
the Ruby Prince was hailed as a hero. And so Fatima and the
Ruby Prince were married and lived happily together. However,
as time passed, Fatima became more and more curious about
her husband's past.

"I know nothing about you," she complained. "At least tell me who you really are and where you once lived!"

But every time the Ruby Prince heard such remarks, he went white and said, "I can't tell you. You mustn't ask, or you'll run the risk of losing me for ever!"

But Fatima was tormented by the desire to know. One day, as they sat by the river that flowed through the Shah's gardens, Fatima pleaded with him to reveal his secret.

White-faced, the young man replied, "I can't!"

But Fatima only pleaded more: "Oh, please! Please tell me!"

"You know I can't . . ."

The Ruby Prince hesitated, gazing at his dearly loved wife and gently stroking her hair. Then he made his decision.

"I don't want to see you suffer like this. If you really must know, then I'll tell you that I'm . . ."

At the very second he was about to reveal his secret, a huge wave swept him into the river and dragged him under the water.

The horrified Princess rushed vainly along the bank, crying loudly for her husband. But he had vanished. Fatima called the guards and even the Shah himself ran up to comfort her. But the Princess became very depressed, for she knew that her foolish questioning had been the cause of the tragedy. One day, her favourite handmaiden hurried up to her.

"Your Highness!" she exclaimed. "I saw the most amazing thing last night. A host of tiny lights appeared on the river, then a thousand little genies draped the river bank with flowers. Such a handsome young man then began to dance in honour of an old man who seemed to be a king. And beside the king stood a young man with a ruby on his forehead. I thought he was . . ."

Fatima's heart leapt: could the young man with the ruby be her husband?

That night, the Princess and her handmaiden went into the garden and hid behind a tree close to the water's edge. On the stroke of midnight, tiny lights began to twinkle on the river, then a stately old man with a white beard, dressed in a golden robe and holding a sceptre, rose from the water.

In the young man beside the throne, Fatima recognized her husband. Covering her face with her veil, she left her hiding place and gracefully began to dance. Wild applause greeted her at the end. Then from the throne came a voice.

"For such a divine dance, ask us whatever you wish for and it will be granted!"

Fatima tore the veil from her face and cried, "Give me back my husband!"

The old king rose to his feet. "The King of the Waters of Persia gave his word. Take back your husband, the Ruby Prince. But do not forget how you lost him and be wiser in future!"

Then the waters opened once more and closed over the King and his Court, leaving Fatima and the Ruby Prince on the bank, reunited and happy at last.

Once upon a time . . .

. . . there was a very naughty wolf who wanted to eat three little pigs but the cleverest of the little pigs was more cunning than the wolf and this is their story . . .

THE THREE LITTLE PIGS

Once upon a time . . . there were three little pigs, who left their mummy and daddy to see the world.

All summer long, they roamed through the woods and over the plains, playing games and having fun. None were happier than the three little pigs, and they easily made friends with everyone. Wherever they went, they were given a warm welcome, but as summer drew to a close, they realized that folk were drifting back to their usual jobs, and preparing for winter. Autumn came and it began to rain. The three little pigs started to feel they needed a real home. Sadly they knew that the fun was over now and they must set to work like the others, or they'd be left in the cold and rain, with no roof over their heads. They talked about what to do, but each decided for himself. The laziest little pig said he'd build a straw hut.

"It will only take a day," he said. The others disagreed.

"It's too fragile," they said disapprovingly, but he refused to listen. Not quite so lazy, the second little pig went in search of planks of seasoned wood.

"Clunk! Clunk! Clunk!" It took him two days to nail them together. But the third little pig did not like the wooden house.

"That's not the way to build a house!" he said. "It takes time, patience and hard work to build a house that is strong enough to stand up to wind, rain, and snow, and most of all, protect us from the wolf!"

The days went by, and the wisest little pig's house took shape, brick by brick. From time to time, his brothers visited him, saying with a chuckle:

"Why are you working so hard? Why don't you come and play?" But the stubborn bricklayer pig just said "no".

"I shall finish my house first. It must be solid and sturdy. And *then* I'll come and play!" he said. "I shall not be foolish like you! For he who laughs last, laughs longest!"

It was the wisest little pig that found the tracks of a big wolf in the neighbourhood.

The little pigs rushed home in alarm. Along came the wolf, scowling fiercely at the laziest pig's straw hut.

"Come out!" ordered the wolf, his mouth watering. "I want to speak to you!"

"I'd rather stay where I am!" replied the little pig in a tiny voice.

"I'll make you come out!" growled the wolf angrily, and puffing out his chest, he took a very deep breath. Then he blew with all his might, right onto the house. And all the straw the silly pig had heaped against some thin poles, fell down in the great blast. Excited by his own cleverness, the wolf did not notice that the little pig had slithered out from underneath the heap of straw, and was dashing towards his brother's wooden house.

When he realized that the little pig was escaping, the wolf grew wild with rage.

"Come back!" he roared, trying to catch the pig as he ran into the wooden house. The other little pig greeted his brother, shaking like a leaf.

"I hope this house won't fall down! Let's lean against the door so he can't break in!"

Outside, the wolf could hear the little pigs' words. Starving as he was, at the idea of a two-course meal, he rained blows on the door.

"Open up! Open up! I only want to speak to you!"
Inside, the two brothers wept in fear and did their best to hold the door fast against the blows. Then the furious wolf braced himself for a new effort: he drew in a really enormous breath, and went . . . WHOOOOO! The wooden house collapsed like a pack of cards.

Luckily, the wisest little pig had been watching the scene from the window of his own brick house, and he rapidly opened the door to his fleeing brothers. And not a moment too soon, for the wolf was already hammering furiously on the door. This time, the wolf had grave doubts. This house had a much more solid air

than the others. He blew once, he blew again and then for a third time. But all was in vain. For the house did not budge an inch. The three little pigs watched him and their fear began to fade. Quite exhausted by his efforts, the wolf decided to try one of his tricks. He scrambled up a nearby ladder, on to the roof to have a look at the chimney. However, the wisest little pig had seen this ploy, and he quickly said:

"Quick! Light the fire!" With his long legs thrust down the chimney, the wolf was not sure if he should slide down the black hole. It wouldn't be easy to get in, but the sound of the little pigs' voices below only made him feel hungrier.

"I'm dying of hunger! I'm going to try and get down." And he let himself drop. But his landing was rather hot, too hot! The wolf landed in the fire, stunned by his fall.

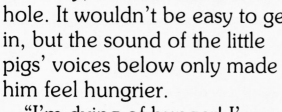

The flames licked his hairy coat and his tail became a flaring torch.

"Never again! Never again will I go down a chimney!" he squealed, as he tried to put out the flames in his tail. Then he ran away as fast as he could.

The three happy little pigs, dancing round and round the yard, began to sing:

"Tra-la-la! Tra-la-la! The wicked black wolf will never come back. . . !"

From that terrible day on, the wisest little pig's brothers set to work with a will. In less than no time, up went the two new brick houses. The wolf did return once to roam in the neighbourhood,

but when he caught sight of *three* chimneys, he remembered the terrible pain of a burnt tail, and he left for good.

Now safe and happy, the wisest little pig called to his brothers: "No more work! Come on, let's go and play!"

THE CRAB AND THE HERON

Once upon a time . . . an elderly heron made his home in a pond full of fish. He was stiff and slow in his old age, and he didn't find it easy to catch his lunch.

However, he decided to use his wits: he went to see a crab, said to be a great chatterbox, and in a mock frightened voice, told him the latest rumour.

"Certain birds, friends of mine, say that the lakeside fishermen will be coming here soon with their nets. They're going to take away all the fish. I'll have no meals left. Everything will be gone and the fish will end up in the frying pan!"

The crab quickly scuttled away to the banks of the pond and dived in to tell the fish the awful news. The frightened fish begged the crab for good advice, and he returned to the heron.

". . . they're all scared stiff and don't know which way to turn. While you yourself snap up a few now and again, it's against your interests if they go. So what shall we do?" The heron pretended to be lost in thought. Then he said: "I'll tell you what! I can carry them, a few at a time, to a pond hidden in the forest. They'll be

quite safe there. But will the fish trust me?"

Whether they were scared of the fishermen, or maybe the crab had a glib tongue, at any rate, the fish agreed to this strange offer. The heron began his trips between pond and forest. But the crab noticed that the heron made excuses for dallying on the way. What was more, the crab's keen eye noticed that the heron's tummy was now a good deal plumper. Days later, when all the fish had been rescued from the pond, the heron said to the crab: "Don't you want to be rescued too?" he asked.

"Certainly!" replied the crab.

"Bend over. I'll climb on to your neck. I'd hate to make your beak tired!"

When they were far from the pond, the crab saw that the ground was littered with fish bones. He clung tightly to the heron's neck with his strong pincers, and said: "I've no intention of coming to the same bad end as the fish! Now, just deposit me gently into the water. I'm not letting go of your neck till I feel safe!"

And from that day on, crabs and herons have always loathed each other and try to avoid meeting.

THE WOLF AND THE SEVEN KIDS

Once upon a time . . . a Mother Goat lived in a pretty little house with her seven kids. Mother often had to leave home to do the shopping, and on that fateful day, she had given her children the usual warnings, before setting off to market.

"You mustn't open the door to anyone. Don't forget, there's a wicked wolf lurking about here. It's black, with horrible paws and a nasty deep voice. If it knocks, keep the door tightly shut!" Mother Goat's words were wise indeed, for as she was telling one of her neighbours about her fears, the wolf disguised as a peasant, was hiding close by, listening to every word.

"Good! Very good!" said the wolf to himself. "If the goat goes to market, I'll drop by her house and gobble the kids!" Then, trying

not to look too conspicuous, the wolf hurried along to the goat's house. There, he threw off his disguise. He then growled in a deep voice: "Open the door! Open the door! It's Mother! I've just come back from market! Open the door!" When the kids heard the deep voice, they remembered their mother's warning. From behind the barred door, they said to the wolf: "We know who you are! You're the wolf! Our mother has a sweet gentle voice, not a deep nasty one like yours! Go away! We'll never open the door to you!"

And though the wolf banged furiously on the door, the kids, though trembling with terror, refused to let him into the house, and so the door remained shut. Then the wolf had a brainwave. He dashed off to the baker's and got a big

cake dripping with honey. He hoped this would sweeten his voice. And in fact, after eating it, his voice didn't sound quite so deep. Over and over again, he practised imitating Mother Goat's voice. You see, he'd heard it in the woods. When he felt certain he could easily be mistaken for Mother Goat herself, he rushed back to the house and the seven kids.

"Open the door! Open the door! It's Mother! I've just come back from market! Open the door!" he called. This time, the kids had doubts: the voice *did* rather sound like mother's, and they were about to unlock the door, when the black kid suspiciously cried: "Mother, let us see your foot!" Without thinking, the wolf raised a black hairy paw. And the kids knew that the wolf had come back.

"You're not our mother! She doesn't have horrid black paws!" cried the kids. "Go away, you wicked wolf!"

And once more, in spite of all his hard work, the wolf

found the door locked against him. The wolf ran down to the mill, and found a sack of flour. He thrust his paws into it until they were pure white.

"I'll trick them this time," he said. "Mmm! My mouth's watering already! I'm hungry! My tummy's empty and my trousers are falling off! I'll swallow these tender kids whole!" Again he knocked on the door.

"Open the door! Open the door! It's Mother! I've just come back from market! Open the door!" The voice seemed exactly like mother's, but the wary kids quickly called out: "Mother, let us see your foot!" The wily wolf lifted a snow white paw, and the kids, now reassured, threw

open the door. What a shock they received! An enormous set of jaws with sharp fangs growled fiercely. Cruel claws reached out for their prey. The kids scattered in terror. One dived under the table, while another crawled below the bed. Another kid hid in the cupboard and one tried to hide in the oven, though the stove was still hot. One kid crouched inside a barrel and one hid in the grandfather clock. There he huddled, holding his breath, as the wolf hunted down his brothers. One by one, the kids were pulled from their hiding places. All except for the kid in the clock. The wicked wolf's appetite did not pass until he had found them and swallowed each in a single gulp.

The only one to escape was the little black kid, for the wolf never imagined that there was room for a kid inside the very narrow grandfather clock. In the meantime, Mother Goat had really come back from market. When, from a distance, she noticed that the door was

ajar, she rushed home, her heart in her mouth. She had a sinking feeling: what she feared had really happened. The wicked wolf had gobbled up all her children. She dropped into a chair, sobbing bitterly, but as she cried, the door of the grandfather clock swung open and out ran the black kid.

"Mummy! Mummy!" wept the kid. "It was terrible! The wolf came, and I think he's eaten all my brothers!"

"My poor child!" sobbed Mother Goat. "You're the only one left! That evil brute has gobbled them all!"

Not long after, Mother Goat and her son left the house to take a stroll in the garden. Suddenly, she heard a low wheezing sound: someone was snoring heavily. It was the greedy wolf. His feast of kids had been too much for him and he was fast asleep, dead to the world. In a flash, Mother Goat had a brainwave. She said to her son: "Run and fetch me a needle and thread and a pair of scissors!" With these, she swiftly slit open the wolf's stomach. As she had hoped, the ravenous brute had swallowed every kid whole. There they were, all still alive inside his tummy. One by one, out they popped from the wolf's tummy.

"Hurry! Hurry! Not a sound! We must get away before he wakens up! Wait! Fetch me a heap of stones!" And so they filled the wolf's stomach with stones and stitched it up again. The wolf woke later with a raging thirst.

"What a heavy tummy I have!" he said. "I've eaten too much! All these kids!" But when he went down to the river to drink, his tummy full of stones tipped him over and he fell into the water. The weight took him straight to the bottom, and the goat and her kids shrieked with joy as he sank. The wicked wolf was dead and the kids trotted home happily with Mother.

THE COUNTRY MOUSE AND THE TOWN MOUSE

Once upon a time . . . a town mouse, on a trip to the country, met a country mouse. They spent the day together and became friends. The country mouse took his new friend into the meadows and vegetable gardens, making him sample all the good things of the land. Never having seen the beauties of the countryside, the town mouse was thrilled, though the country mouse's plain food wasn't nearly as fine as his own usual meals. To thank his friend for the lovely outing, he invited the country mouse to visit him in the town. And when the country mouse saw the pantry at his friend's house, full of hams, cheese, oil, flour, honey, jam and stacks of other goodies, he stood speechless with surprise.

"I've never seen anything like it! Are all those wonderful things for eating?"

"Of course!" came the reply. "You're my guest, so tuck in!" They began

to feast, while the country mouse tried not to stuff himself. He wanted to taste *everything* before finding his tummy full.

"You're the luckiest mouse I've ever met!" said the country mouse to his town brother. The town mouse was listening with delight to his friend's praise, when suddenly, the sound of heavy footsteps interrupted their feast.

"Run for it!" whispered the town mouse to his friend. They were just in

time: for within an inch of them stood the lady of the house's large foot! What a fright! Luckily, the lady went away and the two mice returned to enjoy their meal, so rudely interrupted.

"It's all right! Come on!" said the town mouse. "Don't worry. She's gone. Now for the honey! It's delicious! Have you ever tasted it?"

"Yes, once, a long time ago," the country mouse lied, trying to sound casual. But when he tasted it, he exclaimed: "Scrumptious! By

the King of Mice! I've never eaten anything so lovely in all my life!"

Suddenly there came the sound of footsteps, this time thumping heavily. The two mice fled. The man of the house had come to fetch some bottles, and when he saw the spilt honey, he groaned: "Those ghastly mice again! I thought I'd got rid of them. I'll send the cat!" And trembling with terror, the mice hid away. This time it was

not only the sudden visit that had given them a fright, it was the man's awful words. The mice were so scared, they held their breath, making no sound. Then, since all remained quiet, they began to feel braver, and picked up enough courage to leave their hidey-hole.

"We can come out now! There's nobody here!" the town mouse whispered.

Suddenly, the pantry door creaked, and the two luckless mice froze in fear. Out of the dim light

glowed a pair of horrid yellow eyes. A large cat was staring round the room in search of its prey. The country mouse and the town mouse tiptoed silently back to their hidey-hole. They wished their pounding hearts would stop beating, for fear of the cat hearing the noise they made. But, as luck would have it, the cat discovered a juicy sausage. Forgetting why his master had sent him into the pantry, he stopped to eat it. No longer hungry, after that, the cat decided that he might as well leave mouse-hunting for another day. Off he padded, to have forty winks elsewhere. Now, as soon as the country mouse realized that all danger was past, he did not lose a second. He hastily shook hands with his friend, saying: Thanks so much for everything! But I must rush off now! I can't stand all these shocks! I'd far rather sit down to a meal of a few acorns in peace, in the country, than face a great spread of delicious food, surrounded by dangers on all sides and with my heart in my mouth!"

THE UGLY DUCKLING

Once upon a time . . . down on an old farm, lived a duck family, and Mother Duck had been sitting on a clutch of new eggs. One nice morning, the eggs hatched and out popped six chirpy ducklings. But one egg was bigger than the rest, and it didn't hatch. Mother Duck couldn't recall laying that seventh egg. How did it get there? TOCK! TOCK! The little prisoner was pecking inside his shell.

"Did I count the eggs wrongly?" Mother Duck wondered. But before she had time to think about it, the last egg finally hatched. A strange looking duckling with grey feathers that should have been yellow gazed at a worried mother. The ducklings grew quickly, but Mother Duck had a secret worry.

"I can't understand how this ugly duckling can be one of mine!" she said to herself, shaking her head as she looked at her lastborn. Well, the grey duckling certainly wasn't pretty, and since he ate far more than his brothers, he was outgrowing them. As the days went by, the poor ugly duckling became more and more unhappy. His brothers didn't want to play with him, he was so clumsy, and all the farmyard folks simply laughed at him. He felt sad and lonely, while Mother Duck did her best to console him.

"Poor little ugly duckling!" she would say. "Why are you so different from the others?" And the ugly duckling felt worse than ever. He secretly wept at night. He felt nobody wanted him.

"Nobody loves me, they all tease me! Why am I different from my brothers?"

Then one day, at sunrise, he ran away from the farmyard. He stopped at a pond and began to

question all the other birds: "Do you know of any ducklings with grey feathers like mine?" But everyone shook their heads in scorn.

"We don't know anyone as ugly as you." The ugly duckling did not lose heart, however, and kept on making enquiries. He went

to another pond, where a pair of large geese gave him the same answer to his question. What's more, they warned him: "Don't stay here! Go away! It's dangerous. There are men with guns around here!" The duckling was sorry he had ever left the farmyard.

Then one day, his travels took him near an old countrywoman's cottage. Thinking he was a stray goose, she caught him.

"I'll put this in a hutch. I hope it's a female and lays plenty of eggs!" said the old woman, whose eyesight was poor. But the ugly duckling laid not a single egg. The hen kept frightening him:

"Just wait! If you don't lay eggs, the old woman will wring your neck and pop you into the pot!" And the cat chipped in: "Hee! Hee! I hope the woman cooks you soon, then I can gnaw at your bones!" The poor ugly duckling was so scared that he lost his appetite, though the old woman kept stuffing him with food and grumbling: "If you won't lay eggs, at least hurry up and get plump!"

"Oh, dear me!" moaned the now terrified duckling. "I'll die of fright first! And I did so hope someone would love me!"

Then one night, finding the hutch door ajar, he escaped. Once again he was all alone. He fled as far away as he could, and at dawn, he found himself in a thick bed of reeds. "If nobody wants me, I'll hide here forever." There was plenty of food, and the duckling began to feel a little happier, though he was lonely. One day at sunrise, he saw a flight of beautiful birds wing overhead. White, with long slender necks, yellow beaks and large wings, they were migrating south.

"If only I could look like them, just for a day!" said the duckling, admiringly. Winter came and the water in the reed bed froze. The poor duckling left home to seek food in the snow. He dropped exhausted to the ground, but a farmer found him and put him in his big jacket pocket.

"I'll take him home to my children. They'll look after him. Poor thing, he's frozen!" The duckling was showered with kindly care at the farmer's house. In this way, the ugly duckling was able to survive the bitterly cold winter.

However, by springtime, he had grown so big that the farmer decided: "I'll set him free by the pond!" That was when the duckling saw himself mirrored in the water.

"Goodness! How I've changed! I hardly recognize myself!" The flight of swans winged north again and glided on to the pond. When the duckling saw them, he realized he was one of their kind, and soon made friends.

"We're swans like you!" they said, warmly. "Where have you been hiding?"

"It's a long story," replied the young swan, still astounded. Now, he swam majestically with his fellow swans. One day, he heard children on the river bank exclaim: "Look at that young swan! He's the finest of them all!"

And he almost burst with happiness.

THE STORY OF THUMBELINA

Once upon a time . . . there lived a woman who had no children. She dreamed of having a little girl, but time went by, and her dream never came true.

She then went to visit a witch, who gave her a magic grain of barley. She planted it in a flower pot. And the very next day, the grain had turned into a lovely flower, rather like a tulip. The woman softly kissed its half-shut petals. And as though by magic, the flower opened in full blossom. Inside sat a tiny girl, no bigger than a thumb. The woman called her Thumbelina. For a bed she had a walnut shell, violet petals for her mattress and a rose petal blanket. In the daytime, she played in a tulip petal boat, floating on a plate of water. Using two horse hairs as oars, Thumbelina sailed around her little lake, singing and singing in a gentle sweet voice.

Then one night, as she lay fast asleep in her walnut shell, a large frog hopped through a hole in the window pane. As she gazed down at Thumbelina, she said to herself: "How pretty she is! She'd make the perfect bride for my own dear son!"

She picked up Thumbelina, walnut shell and all, and hopped into the garden. Nobody saw her go. Back at the pond, her fat ugly son, who always did as mother told him, was pleased with her choice. But mother frog was afraid that her pretty prisoner might run away. So she carried Thumbelina out to a water lily leaf in the middle of the pond.

"She can never escape us now," said the frog to her son.

"And we have plenty of time to prepare a new home for you and your bride." Thumbelina was left all alone. She felt so desperate. She knew she would never be able to escape the fate that awaited her with the two horrid fat frogs. All she could do was cry her eyes out. However, one or two minnows who had been enjoying the shade below the water lily leaf, had overheard the two frogs talking, and the little girl's bitter sobs. They decided to do

something about it. So they nibble away at the lily stem till it broke an drifted away in the weak current. A dancing butterfly had an idea: "Throw me the end of your belt! I'l help you to move a little faster!" Thumbelina gratefully did so, and the leaf soon floated away from the frog pond.

But other dangers lay ahead. A large beetle snatched Thumbelina with his strong feet and took her away to his home at the top of a leafy tree.

"Isn't she pretty?" he said to his friends. But they pointed out that she was far too different. So the beetle took her down the tree and set her free.

It was summertime, and Thumbelina wandered all by herself amongst the flowers and through the long grass. She had pollen for her meals and drank the dew. Then the rainy season came, bringing nasty weather. The poor child found it hard to find food and shelter. When winter set in, she suffered from the cold and felt terrible pangs of hunger.

One day, as Thumbelina roamed helplessly over the bare meadows, she met a large spider who promised to help her. He took her to a hollow tree and guarded the door with a stout web. Then he brought her some dried chestnuts and called his friends to come and admire her beauty. But just like the beetles, all the other spiders persuaded Thumbelina's rescuer to let her go. Crying her heart out, and quite certain that nobody wanted her because she was ugly, Thumbelina left the spider's house.

As she wandered, shivering with the cold, suddenly she came across a solid little cottage, made of twigs and dead leaves. Hopefully, she knocked on the door. It was opened by a field mouse.

"What are you doing outside in this weather?" he asked. "Come in and warm yourself." Comfortable and cozy, the field mouse's home was stocked with food. For her keep, Thumbelina did the housework and told the mouse stories. One day, the field mouse said a friend was coming to visit them.

"He's a very rich mole, and has a lovely house. He wears a splendid black fur coat, but he's dreadfully shortsighted.

He needs company and he'd like to marry you!" Thumbelina did not relish the idea. However, when the mole came, she sang sweetly to him and he fell head over heels in love. The mole invited Thumbelina and the field mouse to visit him, but . . . to their surprise and horror, they came upon a swallow in the tunnel. It looked dead. Mole nudged it with his foot, saying: "That'll teach her! She should have come underground instead of darting about the sky all summer!" Thumbelina was so shocked by such cruel words that later, she crept back unseen to the tunnel.

And every day, the little girl went to nurse the swallow and tenderly give it food.

In the meantime, the swallow told Thumbelina its tale. Jagged by a thorn, it had been unable to follow its companions to a warmer climate.

"It's kind of you to nurse me," it told Thumbelina. But, in spring, the swallow flew away, after offering to take the little girl with it. All summer, Thumbelina did her best to avoid marrying the mole. The little girl thought fearfully of how she'd have to live underground forever. On the eve of her wedding, she asked to spend a day in the open air. As she gently fingered a flower, she heard a familiar song: "Winter's on its way and I'll be off to warmer lands. Come with me!" Thumbelina quickly clung to her swallow friend, and the bird soared into the sky. They flew over plains and hills till they reached a country of flowers. The swallow gently laid Thumbelina in a blossom. There she met a tiny, white-winged fairy: the King of the Flower Fairies. Instantly, he asked her to marry him. Thumbelina eagerly said "yes", and sprouting tiny white wings, she became the Flower Queen!

THE ADVENTURES OF TOM THUMB

Once upon a time . . . there lived a giant who had quarrelled with a very greedy wizard over sharing a treasure. After the quarrel, the giant said menacingly to the wizard:

"I could crush you under my thumb if I wanted to! Now, get out of my sight!" The wizard hurried away, but from a safe distance, he hurled his terrible revenge.

"Abracadabra! Here I cast this spell! May the son, your wife will shortly give you, never grow any taller than my own thumb!"

After Tom Thumb was born, his parents were at their wits' end. They could never find him, for they could barely *see* him. They had to speak in whispers for fear of deafening the little boy. Tom Thumb preferred playing with the little garden creatures, to the company of parents so different from himself. He rode piggyback on the snail and danced with the ladybirds. Tiny as he was, he had great fun in the world of little things.

But one unlucky day, he went to visit a froggy friend. No sooner had he scrambled onto a leaf than a large pike swallowed him up. But the pike too was fated to come to a very bad end. A

little later, he took the bait cast by one of the King's fishermen, and before long, found himself under the cook's knife in the royal kitchens. And great was everyone's surprise when, out of the fish's stomach, stepped Tom Thumb, quite alive and little the worse for his adventure.

"What am I to do with this tiny lad?" said the cook to himself. Then he had a brainwave. "He can be a royal pageboy! He's so tiny, I can pop him into the cake I'm making. When he marches across the bridge, sounding the trumpet, everyone will gasp in wonder!" Never had such a marvel been seen at Court. The guests clapped excitedly at the cook's skill and the King himself clapped loudest of all. The King rewarded the clever cook with a bag of gold. Tom Thumb was even luckier. The cook made him a pageboy, and a pageboy he remained, enjoying all the honours of his post.

He had a white mouse for a mount, a gold pin for a sword and he was allowed to eat the King's food. In exchange, he marched up and down the table at banquets. He picked his way amongst the plates and glasses, amusing the guests with his trumpet.

What Tom Thumb didn't know was that he had made an enemy. The cat which, until Tom's arrival, had been the King's pet, was now forgotten. And, vowing to have its revenge on the newcomer, it ambushed Tom in the garden. When Tom saw the cat, he did not run away, as the creature had intended. He whipped out his gold pin and cried to his white mouse mount:

"Charge! Charge!" Jabbed by the tiny sword, the cat turned tail and fled. Since brute force was

not the way to revenge, the cat decided to use guile. Casually pretending to bump into the King as he walked down the staircase, the cat softly miaowed:

"Sire! Be on your guard! A plot is being hatched against your life!" And then he told a dreadful lie. "Tom Thumb is planning to lace your food with hemlock. I saw him picking the leaves in the garden the other day. I heard him say these very words!"

Now, the King had once been kept in bed with very bad tummy pains, after eating too many cherries and he feared the thought of being poisoned, so he sent for Tom

Thumb. The cat provided proof of
his words by pulling a hemlock leaf
from under the white mouse's
saddle cloth, where he had hidden
it himself.

Tom Thumb was so amazed, he
was at a loss for words to deny
what the cat had said. The King,
without further ado, had him
thrown into prison. And since he
was so tiny, they locked him up in a
pendulum clock. The hours passed
and the days too. Tom's only
pastime was swinging back and
forth, clinging to the pendulum,
until the night when he attracted the attention of a big night moth,
fluttering round the room.

"Let me out!" cried Tom Thumb, tapping on the glass. As it so
happens, the moth had only just been set free after being a prisoner in a
large box, in which she had taken a nap. So she took pity on Tom Thumb
and released him.

"I'll take you to the Butterfly Kingdom, where everyone's tiny like
yourself. They'll take care of you there!" And that is what happened. To
this day, if you visit the Butterfly Kingdom, you can ask to see the
butterfly monument that Tom Thumb built after this amazing adventure.

GOLDILOCKS
AND THE
THREE BEARS

Once upon a time . . . in a large forest, close to a village, stood the cottage where the Teddy Bear family lived. They were not really proper Teddy Bears, for Father Bear was very big, Mother Bear was middling in size, and only Baby Bear could be described as a *Teddy* Bear.

Each bear had its own size of bed. Father Bear's was large and nice and comfy. Mother Bear's bed was middling in size, while Baby Bear had a fine little cherrywood bed that Father Bear had ordered from a couple of beaver friends.

Beside the fireplace, around which the family sat in the evenings, stood a large carved chair for the head of the house, a delightful blue velvet armchair for Mother Bear, and a very little chair for Baby Bear.

Neatly laid out on the kitchen table stood three china bowls. A large one for Father Bear, a smaller one for Mother Bear, and a little bowl for Baby Bear.

The neighbours were all very respectful to Father Bear and people raised their hats when he went by. Father Bear liked that and he always politely replied to their greetings. Mother Bear had lots of friends. She visited them in the afternoons to exchange good advice and recipes for jam and bottled fruit. Baby Bear, however, had hardly any friends. This was partly because he was rather a bully and liked to win games and arguments. He was a pest too and always getting into mischief. Not far away, lived a fair-haired little girl who had a similar nature to Baby Bear, only she was haughty and stuck-up as well, and though Baby Bear often asked her to come and play at his house, she always said no.

One day, Mother Bear made a nice pudding. It was a new recipe, with blueberries and other crushed berries. Her friends told her it was delicious. When it was ready, she said to the family:

"It has to be left to cool now, otherwise it won't taste nice. That will take at least an hour. Why don't we go and visit the Beavers' new baby? Mummy Beaver will be pleased to see us." Father Bear and Baby Bear would much rather have tucked into the pudding, warm or not, but they liked the thought of visiting the new baby.

"We must wear our best clothes, even for such a short visit. Everyone at the Beavers' will be very busy now, and we must not stay too long!" And so they set off along the pathway towards the river bank. A short time later, the stuck-up little girl, whose name was Goldilocks, passed by the Bears' house as she picked flowers.

"Oh, what an ugly house the Bears have!" said Goldilocks to herself as she went down the hill. "I'm going to peep inside! It won't be beautiful like my house, but I'm dying to see where Baby Bear lives." Knock! Knock! The little girl tapped on the door. Knock! Knock! Not a sound . . .

"Surely someone will hear me knocking," Goldilocks said to herself, impatiently. "Anyone at home?" she called, peering round the door. Then she went into the empty house and started to explore the kitchen.

"A pudding!" she cried, dipping a finger into the pudding Mother Bear had left to cool. "Quite nice! Quite nice!" she murmured, spooning it from Baby Bear's bowl. In a twinkling, the bowl lay empty on a messy table. With a full tummy, Goldilocks went on exploring.

"Now then, this must be Father Bear's chair, this will be Mother Bear's, and this one . . . must belong to my friend, Baby Bear. I'll just sit on it a while!" With these words, Goldilocks sat herself down onto the little chair which, quite unused to such a sudden weight, promptly broke a leg. Goldilocks crashed to the floor, but not in the least dismayed by the damage she had done, she went upstairs.

There was no mistaking which was Baby Bear's bed.

"Mm! Quite comfy!" she said, bouncing on it. "Not as nice as mine, but nearly!" Then she yawned. "I think I'll lie down, only for a minute . . . just to try the bed." And in next to no time, Goldilocks lay fast asleep in Baby Bear's bed. In the meantime, the Bears were on their way home.

"Wasn't the new Beaver baby ever so small?" said Baby Bear to his mother. "Was I as tiny as that when I was born?"

"Not quite, but almost," came the reply, with a fond caress. From a distance, Father Bear noticed the door was ajar.

"Hurry!" he cried. "Someone is in our house . . ." Was Father Bear hungry or did a thought strike him? Anyway, he dashed into the kitchen. "I knew it! Somebody has gobbled up the pudding . . ."

"Someone has been jumping up and down on my armchair!" complained Mother Bear.

". . . and somebody's broken my chair!" wailed Baby Bear.

Where could the culprit be? They all ran upstairs and tiptoed in amazement over to Baby Bear's bed. In it lay Goldilocks, sound asleep. Baby Bear prodded her toe . . .

"Who's that? Where am I?" shrieked the little girl, waking with a start. Taking fright at the scowling faces bending over her, she clutched the bedclothes up to her chin. Then she jumped out of bed and fled down the stairs.

"Get away! Away from that house!" she told herself as she ran, forgetful of all the trouble she had so unkindly caused. But Baby Bear called from the door, waving his arm:

"Don't run away! Come back! I forgive you . . . come and play with me!"

And this is how it all ended. From that day onwards, haughty rude Goldilocks became a pleasant little girl. She made friends with Baby Bear and often went to his house. She invited him to her house too, and they remained good friends, always.

THE HARE AND THE PORCUPINE

Once upon a time . . . an old porcupine lived in a large wood with his twin sons. Apples were their favourite dish, but the youngsters sometimes raided a neighbouring vegetable plot for the turnips Dad loved to munch. One day, one of the young porcupines set off as usual to fetch the turnips. Like all porcupines, he was a slow walker, and he had just reached a large cabbage, when from behind the leaves, out popped a hare.

"So you have arrived at last!" said the hare. "I've been watching you for half an hour. Do you always dawdle? I hope you're quicker at eating, or it will take you a year to finish the turnips!" Instead of going into a huff at being teased, the porcupine decided to get his own back

by being very crafty.

Slow on his feet but a quick thinker, he rapidly hit on a plan. So the hare sneered at the slow porcupine, did he? Well, the hare's own turn of speed would be his downfall!

"I can run faster than you if I try," said the porcupine. "Ha! Ha!" the hare shrieked with laughter, raising a large paw. "You can't compete with this! My grandad was the speediest hare of his day. He even won a gold penny. He used to be my coach. And you tell me you can run faster than me? Well, I bet my grandad's gold penny that I can win without even trying!"

The porcupine paid little heed to the hare's boastful words and quietly accepted the challenge. "I'll meet you tomorrow down at the ploughed field. We'll race in parallel furrows. And see who wins!"

The hare went away laughing.

"Better stay here all night! You'll never get home and back in time for the race!" he told the porcupine. The porcupine, however, had a bright idea. When he arrived home, he told his twin brother what had happened. Just before dawn next day, he gave him his instructions, and off they set for the

143

field. Hare appeared, rudely remarking: "I'll take off my jacket so I can run faster!"

Ready! Steady! Go! And in a flash, the hare streaked to the other end of the field. There, waiting for him was a porcupine, which teasingly said:

"Rather late, aren't you? I've been here for ages!" Gasping and so breathless his throat was dry, the hare whispered: "Let's try again!"

"All right," agreed the porcupine, "we'll run the race again." Never in all his life had the hare run so fast. Not even with the hounds snapping at his heels. But every time he reached the other end of the ploughed field, what did he find but the porcupine, who laughingly exclaimed: "What? Late again? I keep on getting here first!" Racing up and down the field, the hare sped, trying to beat the porcupine. His legs grew terribly tired and he began to sag. And every time he came to the end of the field, there stood a porcupine calling himself the winner.

"Perhaps I ought to mention, friend hare, that my grandad was the fastest porcupine of his day. He didn't win a gold

penny, but he won apples, and after the race, he ate them. But I don't want apples. I'd rather have the nice gold penny you promised me!" said one of the porcupine twins.

The hare slid to the ground, dead tired. His head was spinning and his legs felt like rubber.

"This race is the end of me! I shall die here in this field, where I really believed I was a sprinter! The shame of it! What a disgrace!" The hare staggered home, hot and sticky, to fetch the gold penny that he had never for a moment ever imagined he would lose. His eyes brimming with tears, he handed it over to the porcupines.

"Thank goodness my grandad isn't alive to see this!" he said. "Whatever would he say? After all his coaching, here I am, beaten by a porcupine!"

That evening, a party was held at the porcupines' house. The twins danced triumphantly in turn, waving aloft the gold penny. Father Porcupine brought out his old accordion for the special occasion, and the fun went on all night. As luck would have it, the hare never did find out the secret of how the race had been rigged. Which was just as well! . . .

THE HARE
AND THE ELEPHANT

Once upon a time . . . in the Indian jungle, lived a young elephant whose playmate was a very large hare. In spite of the difference in size, they were great friends and had fun playing strange guessing games. One day, the hare said to his chum:

"Which of us is bigger: you or me?" At that silly question, the little elephant nearly choked on his banana.

"You must be joking!" he exclaimed. "Why, even on tiptoe, you're not as high as my knee!" But the hare went on:

"That's what *you* think! Since *I* say that I'm bigger than you, we need a judge. Don't you agree?"

"Oh, yes," said the elephant in surprise.

"Well, let's go along to the village and see what the Humans have to say. They're the cleverest of all the animals, and the best judges!" As they reached the village, they met some of the villagers.

"Look at that young elephant! Isn't he small?" folk remarked as the unusual couple strolled by.

"Yes, he is indeed! But he'll soon grow up," said

146

others. Then somebody noticed the hare.

"What a huge hare!" they all cried. Now, the hare tried to keep in front of the elephant and puffed out his chest. As he passed, all the villagers exclaimed:

"Look at his paws! And those ears! That's the biggest hare we've ever seen!" When he heard this, the hare turned to his friend, saying,

"We can go home now! That's settled! I'm huge and you're tiny!" The elephant tossed his heavy head. At a loss for words, he knew the hare had won by low cunning. But back on the jungle path, he lifted his foot and said to the hare, walking ahead, "Get out of my way before a tiny elephant crushes a big hare like you!"

Once upon a time . . .

. . . a carpenter, picked up a strange lump of wood one day while mending a table. When he began to chip it, the wood started to moan. This frightened the carpenter and he decided to get rid of it at once, so he gave it to a friend called Geppetto, who wanted to make a puppet. Geppetto, a cobbler, took his lump of wood home, thinking about the name he would give his puppet.

"I'll call him Pinocchio," he told himself. "It's a lucky name."
Back in his humble basement home and workshop, Geppetto
started to carve the wood. Suddenly a voice squealed:

"Ooh! That hurt!" Geppeto was astonished to find that the
wood was alive. Excitedly he carved a head, hair and eyes, which
immediately stared right at the cobbler. But the second Geppetto
carved out the nose, it grew longer and longer, and no matter
how often the cobbler cut it down to size, it just stayed a long
nose. The newly cut mouth began to chuckle and when
Geppetto angrily complained, the puppet stuck out his tongue at
him. That was nothing, however! When the cobbler shaped the
hands, they snatched the good man's wig, and the newly carved
legs gave him a hearty kick. His eyes brimming with tears,
Geppetto scolded the puppet.

"You naughty boy! I haven't even finished making you, yet
you've no respect for your father!" Then he picked up the puppet
and, a step at a time, taught him to walk. But the minute
Pinocchio stood upright, he started to run about the room, with
Geppetto after him, then he opened the door and dashed into
the street. Now, Pinocchio ran faster than Geppetto and though
the poor cobbler shouted "Stop him! Stop him!" none of the
onlookers, watching in amusement, moved a finger. Luckily, a

policeman heard the cobbler's shouts and strode quickly down the street. Grabbing the runaway, he handed him over to his father.

"I'll box your ears," gasped Geppetto, still out of breath. Then he realised that was impossible, for in his haste to carve the puppet, he had forgotten to make his ears. Pinocchio had got a fright at being in the clutches of the police, so he apologised and Geppetto forgave his son.

Indeed, the minute they reached home, the cobbler made Pinocchio a suit out of flowered paper, a pair of bark shoes and a soft bread hat. The puppet hugged his father.

"I'd like to go to school," he said, "to become clever and help you when you're old!" Geppetto was touched by this kind thought.

"I'm very grateful," he replied, "but we haven't enough money even to buy you the first reading book!" Pinocchio looked downcast, then Geppetto suddenly rose to his feet, put on his old tweed coat and went out of the house. Not long after he returned carrying a first reader, but minus his coat. It was snowing outside.

"Where's your coat, father?"

"I sold it."

"Why did you sell it?"

"It kept me too warm!"

Pinocchio threw his arms round Geppetto's neck and kissed the kindly old man.

It had stopped snowing and Pinocchio set out for school with his first reading book under his arm. He was full of good intentions. "Today I want to learn to read. Tomorrow I'll learn to write and the day after to count. Then I'll earn some money and buy Geppetto a fine new coat. He deserves it, for . . ." The sudden sound of a brass band broke into the puppet's daydream and he soon forgot all about school. He ended up in a crowded square where people were clustering round a brightly coloured booth.

"What's that?" he asked a boy.

"Can't you read? It's the Great Puppet Show!"

"How much do you pay to go inside?"

"Fourpence."

"Who'll give me fourpence for this brand new book?" Pinocchio cried. A nearby junk seller bought the reading book and Pinocchio hurried into the booth. Poor Geppetto. His sacrifice had been quite in vain. Hardly had Pinocchio got inside, when he was seen by one of the puppets on the stage who cried out:

"There's Pinocchio! There's Pinocchio!"

"Come along. Come up here with us. Hurrah for brother Pinocchio!" cried the puppets. Pinocchio went onstage with his new friends, while the spectators below began to mutter about

the uproar. Then out strode Giovanni, the puppet-master, a frightful looking man with fierce bloodshot eyes.

"What's going on here? Stop that noise! Get in line, or you'll hear about it later!"

That evening, Giovanni sat down to his meal, but when he found that more wood was needed to finish cooking his nice chunk of meat, he remembered the intruder who had upset his show.

"Come here, Pinocchio! You'll make good firewood!" The poor puppet started to weep and plead.

"Save me, father! I don't want to die . . . I don't want to die!" When Giovanni heard Pinocchio's cries, he was surprised.

"Are your parents still alive?" he asked.

"My father is, but I've never known my mother," said the puppet in a low voice. The big man's heart melted.

"It would be beastly for your father if I did throw you into the fire . . . but I must finish roasting the mutton. I'll just have to burn another puppet. Men! Bring me Harlequin, trussed!" When Pinocchio saw that another puppet was going to be burned in his place, he wept harder than ever.

"Please don't, sir! Oh, sir, please don't! Don't burn Harlequin!"

"That's enough!" boomed Giovanni in a rage. "I want my meat well cooked!"

"In that case," cried Pinocchio defiantly, rising to his feet, "burn me! It's not right that Harlequin should be burnt instead of me!"

Giovanni was taken aback. "Well, well!" he said. "I've never met a puppet hero before!" Then he went on in a milder tone. "You really are a good lad. I might indeed . . ." Hope flooded Pinocchio's heart as the puppet-master stared at him, then at last the man said: "All right! I'll eat half-raw mutton tonight, but next time, somebody will find himself in a pickle." All the puppets were delighted at being saved. Giovanni asked Pinocchio to tell him the whole tale, and feeling sorry for kindhearted Geppetto, he gave the puppet five gold pieces.

"Take these to your father," he said. "Tell him to buy himself a new coat, and give him my regards."

Pinocchio cheerfully left the puppet booth after thanking Giovanni for being so generous. He was hurrying homewards when he met a half-blind cat and a lame fox. He couldn't help but tell them all about his good fortune, and when the pair set eyes on the gold coins, they hatched a plot, saying to Pinocchio:

"If you would really like to please your

father, you ought to take him a lot more coins. Now, we know of a magic meadow where you can sow these five coins. The next day, you will find they have become ten times as many!"

"How can that happen?" asked Pinocchio in amazement.

"I'll tell you how!" exclaimed the fox. "In the land of Owls lies a meadow known as Miracle Meadow. If you plant one gold coin in a little hole, next day you will find a whole tree dripping with gold coins!" Pinocchio drank in every word his two "friends" uttered and off they all went to the Red Shrimp Inn to drink to their meeting and future wealth.

After food and a short rest, they made plans to leave at midnight for Miracle Meadow. However, when Pinocchio was wakened by the innkeeper at the time arranged, he found that the fox and the cat had already left. All the puppet could do then was pay for the dinner, using one of his gold coins, and set off alone along the path through the woods to the magic meadow. Suddenly . . . "Your money or your life!" snarled two hooded bandits. Now, Pinocchio had hidden the coins under his tongue, so he could not say a word, and nothing the bandits could do would make Pinocchio tell where the coins were hidden. Still mute, even when the wicked pair tied a noose round the poor puppet's neck and pulled it tighter and tighter, Pinocchio's last thought was "Father, help me!"

Of course, the hooded bandits were the fox and the cat. "You'll hang there," they said, "till you decide to talk. We'll be back soon to see if you have changed your mind!" And away they went.

However, a fairy who lived nearby had overheard everything . . . From the castle window, the Turquoise Fairy saw a kicking puppet dangling from an oak tree in the wood. Taking pity on him, she clapped

her hands three times and suddenly a hawk and a dog appeared.

"Quickly!" said the fairy to the hawk. "Fly to that oak tree and with your beak snip away the rope round the poor lad's neck!"

To the dog she said: "Fetch the carriage and gently bring him to me!"

In no time at all, Pinocchio, looking quite dead, was lying in a cosy bed in the castle, while the fairy called three famous doctors, crow, owl and cricket. A very bitter medicine, prescribed by these three doctors quickly cured the puppet, then as she caressed him, the fairy said: "Tell me what happened!"

Pinocchio told her his story, leaving out the bit about selling his first reading book, but when the fairy asked him where the gold coins were, the puppet replied that he had lost them. In fact, they were hidden in one of his pockets. All at once, Pinocchio's nose began to stretch, while the fairy laughed.

"You've just told a lie! I know you have, because your nose is growing longer!" Blushing with shame, Pinocchio had no idea what to do with such an ungainly nose and he began to weep. However, again feeling sorry for him, the fairy clapped her hands and a flock of woodpeckers appeared to peck his nose back to its proper length.

"Now, don't tell any more lies," the fairy warned him, "or your nose will grow again! Go home and take these coins to your father."

Pinocchio gratefully hugged the fairy and ran off homewards. But near the oak tree in the forest, he bumped into the cat and the fox. Breaking his promise, he foolishly let himself be talked into burying the coins in the magic meadow. Full of hope, he returned next day, but the coins had gone. Pinocchio sadly trudged home without the coins Giovanni had given him for his father.

After scolding the puppet for his long absence, Geppetto forgave him and off he went to school. Pinocchio seemed to have calmed down a bit. But someone else was about to cross his path and lead him astray. This time, it was Carlo, the lazybones of the class.

"Why don't you come to Toyland with me?" he said. "Nobody ever studies there and you can play all day long!"

"Does such a place really exist?" asked Pinocchio in amazement.

"The wagon comes by this evening to take me there," said Carlo. "Would you like to come?"

Forgetting all his promises to his father and the fairy, Pinocchio was again heading for trouble. Midnight struck, and the wagon arrived to pick up the two friends, along with some other lads who could hardly wait to reach a place where schoolbooks and teachers had never been heard of. Twelve pairs of donkeys pulled the wagon, and they were all shod with white leather boots. The boys clambered into the wagon. Pinocchio, the most excited of them all, jumped on to a donkey. Toyland, here we come!

Now Toyland was just as Carlo had described it: the boys all had great fun and there were no lessons. You weren't even allowed to whisper the word "school", and Pinocchio could hardly believe he was able to play all the time.

"This is the life!" he said each time he met Carlo.

"I was right, wasn't I?" exclaimed his friend, pleased with himself.

"Oh, yes Carlo! Thanks to you I'm enjoying myself. And just think: teacher told me to keep well away from you."

165

One day, however, Pinocchio awoke to a nasty surprise. When he raised a hand to his head, he found he had sprouted a long pair of hairy ears, in place of the sketchy ears that Geppetto had never got round to finishing. And that wasn't all! The next day, they had grown longer than ever. Pinocchio shamefully pulled on a large cotton cap and went off to search for Carlo. He too was wearing a hat, pulled right down to his nose. With the same thought in their heads, the boys stared at each other, then snatching off their hats, they began to laugh at the funny sight of long hairy ears. But as they screamed with laughter, Carlo suddenly went pale and began to stagger. "Pinocchio, help! Help!" But Pinocchio himself was stumbling about and he burst into tears. For their faces were growing into the shape of a donkey's head and they felt themselves go down on all fours. Pinocchio and Carlo were turning into a pair of donkeys. And when they tried to groan with fear, they brayed loudly instead. When the Toyland wagon driver heard the braying of his new donkeys, he rubbed his hands in glee.

"There are two fine new donkeys to take to market. I'll get at least four gold pieces for them!" For such was the awful fate that awaited naughty little boys that played truant from school to spend all their time playing games.

Carlo was sold to a farmer, and a circus man bought Pinocchio to teach him to do tricks like his other performing animals. It was a hard life for a donkey! Nothing to eat but hay, and when that was gone, nothing but straw. And the beatings! Pinocchio was beaten every day till he had mastered the difficult circus tricks. One day, as he was jumping through the hoop, he stumbled and went lame. The circus man called the stable boy.

"A lame donkey is no use to me," he said. "Take it to market and get rid of it at any price!" But nobody wanted to buy a useless donkey. Then along came a little man who said: "I'll take

it for the skin. It will make a good drum for the village band!"

And so, for a few pennies, Pinocchio changed hands and he brayed sorrowfully when he heard what his awful fate was to be. The puppet's new owner led him to the edge of the sea, tied a large stone to his neck, and a long rope round Pinocchio's legs and pushed him into the water. Clutching the end of the rope, the man sat down to wait for Pinocchio to drown. Then he would flay off the donkey's skin.

Pinocchio struggled for breath at the bottom of the sea, and in a flash, remembered all the bother he had given Geppetto, his broken promises too, and he called on the fairy.

The fairy heard Pinocchio's call and when she saw he was about to drown, she sent a shoal of big fish. They ate away all the donkey flesh, leaving the wooden Pinocchio. Just then, as the fish stopped nibbling, Pinocchio felt himself hauled out of the water. And the man gaped in astonishment at the living puppet,

168

twisting and turning like an eel, which appeared in place of the dead donkey. When he recovered his wits, he babbled, almost in tears: "Where's the donkey I threw into the sea?"

"I'm that donkey," giggled Pinocchio.

"You!" gasped the man. "Don't try pulling my leg. If I get angry . . ."

However, Pinocchio told the man the whole story . . . "and that's how you come to have a live puppet on the end of the rope instead of a dead donkey!"

"I don't give a whit for your story," shouted the man in a rage. "All I know is that I paid twenty coins for you and I want my money back! Since there's no donkey, I'll take you to market and sell you as firewood!"

By then free of the rope, Pinocchio made a face at the man and dived into the sea. Thankful to be a wooden puppet again, Pinocchio swam happily out to sea and was soon just a dot on the horizon. But his adventures were far from over. Out of the water behind him loomed a terrible giant shark! A horrified Pinocchio saw its wide open jaws and tried to swim away as fast as he could, but the monster only glided closer. Then the puppet tried to escape by going in the other direction, but in vain. He could never escape the shark, for as the water rushed

into its cavern-like mouth, he was sucked in with it. And in an instant Pinocchio had been swallowed along with shoals of fish unlucky enough to be in the fierce creature's path. Down he went, tossed in the torrent of water as it poured down the shark's throat, till he felt dizzy. When Pinocchio came to his senses, he was in darkness. Over his head, he could hear the loud heave of the shark's gills. On his hands and knees, the puppet crept down what felt like a sloping path, crying as he went:

"Help! Help! Won't anybody save me?"

Suddenly, he noticed a pale light and, as he crept towards it, he saw it was a flame in the distance. On he went, till: "Father! It can't be you! . . ."

"Pinocchio! Son! It really is you . . ."

Weeping for joy, they hugged each other and, between sobs, told their adventures. Geppetto stroked the puppet's head and told him how he came to be in the shark's stomach.

"I was looking for you everywhere. When I couldn't find you on dry land, I made a boat to search for you on the sea. But the boat capsized in a storm, then the

shark gulped me down. Luckily, it also swallowed bits of ships wrecked in the tempest, so I've managed to survive by getting what I could from these!"

"Well, we're still alive!" remarked Pinocchio, when they had finished recounting their adventures. "We must get out of here!" Taking Geppetto's hand, the pair started to climb up the shark's stomach, using a candle to light their way. When they got as far as its jaws, they took fright, but as it so happened, this shark slept with its mouth open, for it suffered from asthma.

"Now's our chance to escape," whispered Pinocchio. In a second he was in the water, swimming as quickly as he could, with Geppetto on his back.

As luck would have it, the shark had been basking in shallow waters since the day before, and Pinocchio soon reached the beach. Dawn was just breaking, and Geppetto, soaked to the skin, was half dead with cold and fright.

"Lean on me, father." said Pinocchio. "I don't know where we are, but we'll soon find our way home!"

Beside the sands stood an old hut made of branches, and there they took shelter. Geppetto was running a temperature, but Pinocchio went out, saying, "I'm going to get you some milk." The bleating of goats led the puppet in the right direction, and he soon came upon a farmer. Of course, he had no money to pay for the milk.

"My donkey's dead," said the farmer. "If you work the treadmill from dawn to noon, then you can have some milk." And so, for days on end, Pinocchio rose early each morning to earn Geppetto's food.

At long last, Pinocchio and Geppetto reached home. The puppet worked late into the night weaving reed baskets to make money for his father and himself. One day, he heard that the fairy after a wave of bad luck, was ill in hospital. So instead of buying himself a new suit of clothes, Pinocchio sent the fairy the money to pay for her treatment.

One night, in a wonderful dream, the fairy appeared to reward Pinocchio for his kindness. When the puppet looked in the mirror next morning, he found he had turned into somebody else. For there in the mirror, was a handsome young lad with blue eyes and brown hair. Geppetto hugged him happily.

"Where's the old wooden Pinocchio?" the young lad asked in astonishment.

"There!" exclaimed Geppetto, pointing at him. "When bad boys become good, their looks change along with their lives!"

WHAT OTHER PEOPLE THINK

Once upon a time . . . a farmer and his son went to market to sell a donkey. However, they loaded the beast into the wheelbarrow, so that it would not reach market tired and worn out, and pushed it along the road. When people saw such a peculiar sight, they loudly remarked: "That man is mad! Whoever saw a donkey being taken to market in a wheelbarrow!"

The poor farmer became more and more confused, for the farther he went, the louder the comments became and the more people gossiped. It was the last straw when, as they passed the blacksmith's forge, the smith jeeringly asked the farmer if he wanted shoeing, since he was doing the donkey work! So the farmer stopped, heaved the animal out of the wheelbarrow and climbed onto its back, while his son walked behind.

But that made matters even worse!

A group of women going home from market instantly complained: "You cruel man! Fancy a great lump like you riding a donkey, while your poor little boy runs along behind! You ought to be ashamed of yourself!"

People heaped insult upon insult, till the unhappy farmer slid off the donkey. He simply did not know what to do next. He took off his cap and mopped his brow.

"Whew!" he exclaimed. "I never imagined it could be so difficult to take a donkey to market."

174

Then he hoisted his little boy onto the donkey and walked along behind. This time, a cluster of men began to protest.

"Look at that! There's a young lad sitting pretty as you please on top of a donkey, while his weary old father has to go on foot!"

"It's a disgrace."

Once again, father and son came to a halt. How on earth could they stop people from criticizing everything they did? Well, in the end, they *both* got on the donkey.

"What heartless folk!" exclaimed the passers-by. "Two riders on one little donkey!" But by now the farmer had lost his patience. He gave the donkey a terrible kick, saying:

"Giddy up! From now on, I'll do things my way, and pay no attention to what other people think!"

CHICO AND THE CRANE

Once upon a time . . . in the city of Florence lived Mr Corrado, a nobleman famous for his love of hunting and for his banquets. One day, his falcon caught a beautiful crane, which Mr Corrado handed to the cook and told him to roast to perfection.

The bird was almost done when a pretty young peasant girl entered the kitchen to visit the cook. When she sniffed the savoury smell of roasting, the girl persuaded Chico to give her one of the bird's legs. In due course, the crane was carried to the nobleman's table and Mr Corrado summoned the cook to explain what had happed to the missing leg. To his question, the unfortunate cook replied:

"Sire! Cranes have only one leg!"

"What? One leg?" exclaimed Mr Corrado. "Do you think I've never seen a crane before?" But Chico insisted that these birds had only one leg: "If I had a live bird here, I'd show you!" However, the nobleman had no desire to argue in front of his guests, but he told the cook:

"Very well. We'll go and see tomorrow morning, but woe betide you if it's not true."

At sunrise, Mr Corrado, angrier than ever, gave the order to saddle the horses. "Now we'll see who's telling lies," he said grimly. Chico would gladly have fled in fear, but he did not dare. However, as they approached the river, the cook spotted a flock of cranes, fast asleep. Of course, they were all standing on one leg, as they do when resting. "Sire! Sire!" Chico cried. "Look, I was right. They have only one leg."

"Indeed!" snorted Mr Corrado. "I'll show you!" And so saying, he clapped his hands and gave a shout. At the sudden sound, the cranes uncurled the other leg and flapped away.

"There you are, you scoundrel," growled the nobleman. "You see they have two legs!" To which Chico quickly retorted, "But Sire, if you had clapped and shouted at table yesterday, then the bird would have uncurled its other leg!"

At such a clever reply, Mr Corrado's anger turned to amusement. "Yes, Chico, you're right. I should have done just that!" And he clapped the cook's shoulder, as they parted friends.

THE THREE WISHES

Once upon a time . . . a woodcutter lived happily with his wife in a pretty little log cabin in the middle of a thick forest. Each morning he set off singing to work, and when he came home in the evening, a plate of hot steaming soup was always waiting for him.

One day, however, he had a strange surprise. He came upon a big fir tree with strange open holes on the trunk. It looked somehow different from the other trees, and just as he was about to chop it down, the alarmed face of an elf popped out of a hole.

"What's all this banging?" asked the elf. "You're not thinking of cutting down this tree, are you? It's my home. I live here!" The

woodcutter dropped his axe in astonishment.

"Well, I . . ." he stammered.

"With all the other trees there are in this forest, you have to pick this one. Lucky I was in, or I would have found myself homeless."

Taken aback at these words, the woodcutter quickly recovered, for after all the elf was quite tiny, while he himself was a big hefty chap, and he boldly replied: "I'll cut down any tree I like, so . . ."

"All right! All right!" broke in the elf. "Shall we put it this way: if you don't cut down *this* tree, I grant you three wishes. Agreed?" The woodcutter scratched his head.

"Three wishes, you say? Yes, I agree." And he began to hack at another tree. As he worked and sweated at his task, the woodcutter kept thinking about the magic wishes.

"I'll see what my wife thinks . . ."

The woodcutter's wife was busily cleaning a pot outside the house when her husband arrived. Grabbing her round the waist, he twirled her in delight.

"Hooray! Hooray! Our luck is in!"

The woman could not understand why her husband was so pleased with himself and she shrugged herself free. Later, however, over a glass of fine wine at the table, the woodcutter told his wife of his meeting with the elf, and she too began to picture the wonderful things that the elf's three wishes might give them. The woodcutter's wife took a first sip of wine from her husband's glass.

"Nice," she said, smacking her lips. "I wish I had a string of sausages to go with it, though . . ."

Instantly she bit her tongue, but too late. Out of the air appeared the sausages, while the woodcutter stuttered with rage.

". . . what have you done! Sausages . . . What a stupid waste of a wish! You foolish woman. I wish they would stick up your nose!" No sooner said than done. For the sausages leapt up and stuck fast to the end of the woman's nose. This time, the woodcutter's wife flew into a rage.

"You idiot, what have *you* done? With all the things we could have wished for . . ." The mortified woodcutter, who had just repeated his wife's own mistake, exclaimed:

"I'd chop . . ." Luckily he stopped himself in time, realizing with horror that he'd been on the point of having his tongue chopped off. As his wife complained and blamed him, the poor man burst out laughing.

"If only you knew how funny you look with those sausages on the end of your nose!" Now that really upset the woodcutter's wife. She hadn't thought of her looks. She tried to tug away the sausages but they would not budge. She pulled again and again, but in vain. The sausages were firmly attached to her nose. Terrified, she exclaimed: "They'll be there for the rest of my life!"

Feeling sorry for his wife and wondering how he could ever put up with a woman with such an awkward nose, the woodcutter said: "I'll try."

Grasping the string of sausages, he tugged with all his might. But he simply pulled his wife over on top of him. The pair sat on the floor, gazing sadly at each other.

"What shall we do now?" they said, each thinking the same thought.

"There's only one thing we *can* do . . ." ventured the woodcutter's wife timidly.

"Yes, I'm afraid so . . ." her husband sighed, remembering their dreams of riches, and he bravely wished the third and last wish: "I wish the sausages would leave my wife's nose."

And they did. Instantly, husband and wife hugged each other tearfully, saying: "Maybe we'll be poor, but we'll be happy again!"

That evening, the only reminder of the woodcutter's meeting with the elf was the string of sausages. So the couple fried them, gloomily thinking of what that meal had cost them.

ALI
AND THE
SULTAN'S SADDLE

Once upon a time . . . there lived a very powerful Sultan whose kingdom stretched to the edges of the desert. One of his subjects was called Ali, a man who enjoyed making fun of his ruler. He invented all sorts of tales about the Sultan and his Court, and folk would roar with laughter at his jokes. Indeed, Ali became so well known, that people pointed him out in the street and chuckled.

Ali's fun at the Sultan's expense reached the point where the Sultan himself heard about it. Angry and insulted, he ordered the guards to bring the joker before him.

"I shall punish him for his cheek," said the Sultan eagerly, as he rubbed his hands, thinking of the good whipping he was about to administer.

But when Ali was brought before him, he bowed so low that his forehead scraped the floor. Giving the Sultan no time to open his mouth, Ali said:

"Sire! Please let me thank you for granting my dearest wish: to look upon you in person and tell you how greatly I admire your wisdom and handsome figure. I've written a poem about you. May I recite it to you?"

Overwhelmed by this stream of words and delighted at Ali's unexpected praise, the Sultan told him to recite his poem. In actual fact, Ali hadn't written a single word, so he had to invent it as he went along, and this he did, loudly comparing the Sultan's splendour to that of the sun, his strength to that of the tempest and his voice to the sound of the wind. Everyone applauded and cheered. Now quite charmed, the Sultan forgot why he had called Ali before him, and clapped at the end of the poem in his honour.

"Well done!" he cried. "You're a fine poet and deserve a reward. Choose one of these saddles as payment for your ability." Ali picked up a donkey's saddle and, thanking the Sultan, he hurried out of the palace with the saddle on his back. When people saw him rush along, they all asked him:

"Ali, where are you going with that donkey's saddle on your back?"

"I've just recited a poem in honour of the Sultan, and he's given me one of his own robes as a reward!"

And winking, Ali pointed to the saddle!

AMIN AND THE EGGS

Once upon a time . . . a peasant called Amin lost all his crops from his miserable little plot in a drought. He decided to seek his fortune in another village, and off he went on his donkey. On credit, he obtained a dozen hard-boiled eggs from a merchant for his journey.

Seven years later, Amin returned to his village. This time he was riding a fine black horse, followed by a servant on a camel laden with gold and silver coins. Amin had become a rich man and the news of this soon spread through the village. Straight away, the merchant who had given him the dozen eggs on credit knocked at Amin's door, asking for five hundred silver pieces in payment of the old debt. Amin of course refused to pay such a large sum and the matter was taken before the judge.

On the day of the hearing, the merchant appeared in court at the appointed time, but of Amin there was no sign. The judge waited impatiently for a quarter of an hour, and was on the point of adjourning the hearing, when Amin dashed in, out of breath. At once, the merchant said, in defence of his demands:

"I asked Amin for payment of five hundred silver coins, because twelve chickens might have hatched from the eggs he bought from me on credit, seven years ago. These chickens

would have become hens and cockerels; more eggs would have been laid, these too would have hatched, and so on. After seven years, I might have had a great flock of fowls!"

"Of course," agreed the judge. "Perfectly right." And turning to Amin with a hostile air, he ordered: "What have you to say for yourself? And, by the way, why are you late?" Amin did not turn a hair.

"I had a plate of boiled beans in the house and I planted them in the garden to have a good crop next year!"

"Fool!" exclaimed the judge. "Since when do boiled beans grow?" To which Amin promptly retorted:

"And since when do boiled eggs hatch into chickens?"

He had won his case.

SALEM AND THE NAIL

Once upon a time . . . the shop belonging to an astute merchant called Salem, and all the carpets in it, were burnt in a fire. Salem was left with nothing but his house, and since he was a trader he decided to sell it. With the money he would be able to buy a new shop and more carpets. Salem did not ask a high price for his house. However, he had a most unusual request to make of would-be buyers: "I'll sell you the house, except for that nail in the wall. That remains mine!" And as they all went off, shaking their heads, they wondered what he meant by this strange remark.

Abraham, however, more miserly than all the others, thought the price was fair, and he even haggled it down further. A bargain was struck and the new owner took over the whole house, except for the nail. A week later, Salem knocked at the door.

"I've come to hang something on my nail," he said. Abraham let him in and Salem hung up a large empty bag, said goodbye and left. A few days later, he appeared again, and this time hung an old cloak on the nail. From then on, Salem's visits became regular; he was forever coming and going, taking things off the nail or hanging something else up.

One evening, in front of the stunned eyes of Abraham and his family, Salem arrived dragging a dead donkey. With a struggle, he hoisted it up and roped it to the nail. The occupants of the house complained about the smell and the sight of the dead beast, but Salem calmly said: "It's my nail and I can hang anything I like on it!"

Abraham, naturally, could no longer live in the house under such conditions. But Salem refused to remove the donkey.

"If you don't like it," he said, "you can get out of my house, but I'll not pay you back a penny!"

Abraham did his best to persuade Salem to take the donkey down, for it smelt to high heaven. He even consulted a judge, but the terms of the bargain were clear. The house belonged to Abraham, but Salem kept the nail.

In the end, Abraham was forced to leave, and Salem got his house back without paying a penny for it!

THE GOLDEN GOOSE

Once upon a time . . . there was a woodcutter called Thaddeus, a dreamy, foolish-looking lad though good-hearted. One day, his father sent him to a distant wood to chop down trees. Thaddeus thought that these trees were a kind he had never seen before and that it was hard work trying to hack through their hard trunks. Sweating after all his efforts, he had barely sat down against a sawn-off trunk to have a meal, when a strange old man with a white beard popped out from behind a bush and asked him for a bite to eat. Kindly Thaddeus gave him some bread and cheese and together they cheerily drank a flask of wine.

"Of all the woodcutters that have tried to fell these trees, you're the first one who has been nice to me," said the old man, stuttering, perhaps after all the wine. "You deserve a reward. If you cut down that tree in the centre of the wood, you'll find that all the others will fall down by themselves. Have a look in its roots where there's a gift for you! You see, I'm the Wizard of the Woods!"

Not particularly surprised, Thaddeus did as he was told, and in a flash, his work was done. From the roots of the tree the Wizard had pointed towards, the woodcutter took a golden goose. Slipping the bird under his arm, Thaddeus set off homewards. Now, it may have been too much wine, or maybe the fact he was new to these parts, but the fact remains that Thaddeus lost his way. At dead of night, he reached a strange village. A tavern was still open, so the woodcutter went in.

"Something to eat for myself and for the Golden Goose that the Wizard of the Woods gave me," he ordered the innkeeper's daughter. "That's a bite for me and a bite for you," he said, sharing his food with the goose across the table. The innkeeper's other two daughters came to stare at the strange sight, then all three dared ask: "Why are you so kind to a goose?"

"This is a magic goose," replied Thaddeus, "and worth a fortune. I shall stay the night here and I need a secure room, for I don't want to be robbed."

However, during the night, one of the sisters was persuaded to steal at least one goose feather.

"If it's a magic bird, then one of its feathers will be precious too!" But the second her hand touched the goose's tail, it stuck fast, and nothing would unstick it. In a low voice, she called her sisters, but when they tried to pull her free, they too stuck fast. A little later, Thaddeus woke, not at all surprised to see the three sisters, ashamed at being discovered, stuck to the golden goose.

"How can we get free?" they wailed. But the woodcutter coolly replied:

"I have to leave with my goose. Too bad for you if you're stuck to her. You'll just have to come too!" And when the innkeeper saw the strange little procession trip past, he shouted "What's up?" and grabbed the last sister by the arm. It was the worst thing he could have done! For he too found himself attached to the tail of the little group. The same fate awaited a nosy village woman, the plump curate and the baker who had placed a hand on the curate's shoulder as he rushed past. Last of all came a guard who had tried to stop the procession. People laughed as Thaddeus and his row of followers went by, and crowds soon flocked the roads.

Close to the village where Thaddeus had spent the night stood the Royal Palace. Though rich and powerful, the King had a great sorrow: his only daughter suffered from a strange illness that no doctor had been able to cure. She was always sad and unhappy. The King had once proclaimed that the man who succeeded in making his daughter laugh would be granted her hand in marriage. But so far, nobody had so much as brought a smile to the Princess's lips.

As it so happened, the Princess chose that day to drive through the village square, just as the woodcutter with the goose under his arm, solemnly marched by with his line of unwilling followers. When she heard the people chuckle, the Princess raised the carriage curtains. The minute she set eyes on the amazing sight, she burst into peals of laughter.

Everyone was amazed to hear the Princess laugh for the first time. She stepped down from the carriage for a closer look at the golden goose and that's how she got stuck to the baker! Laughing and chattering, the procession headed towards the palace, with the crowds at their heels. When the King saw his daughter in fits of laughter, he could hardly believe it.

"How amazing! How amazing!" he said.

But in spite of all the mirth, it was a serious situation. That is, until a large man with a tall peaked hat and a white beard stepped forward and snapped his fingers three times. Suddenly, Thaddeus and the others all became unstuck. The woodcutter was about to thank the Wizard of the Woods, for it could be none other, but he had vanished into thin air. And that's how the simple woodcutter, Thaddeus, found himself married to the King's daughter.

THE MUSICIANS OF BREMEN

Once upon a time . . . an old donkey was ill-treated by his master. Tired of such unkindness, he decided to run away, and when he heard that Bremen was looking for singers with the town band, he decided that someone with a fine braying voice like his might be accepted.

As he went along the road, the donkey met a skinny dog, covered with sores.

"Come with me. If you have a good bark, you'll find a job with the band too. Just wait and see!"

A little later, a stray cat, no longer able to catch mice, joined them and the trio trotted hopefully on towards the town. As they passed a farmyard, they stopped to admire an elderly cockerel who, with outstretched wings, was crowing to the skies.

"You sing well," they told him. "What are you so happy about?"

"Happy?" muttered the cockerel with tears in his eyes. "They want to put me in the pot and make broth of me. I'm singing as hard as I can today, for tomorrow I'll be gone." But the donkey told him, "Run away with us. With a voice like yours, you'll be famous in Bremen!"

Now there were four of them. The way was long, night fell, and very frightened, the four creatures found themselves in a thick forest.

192

They scarcely knew whether to press on or to hide in some caves and rest. Suddenly, in the distance they saw a light amongst the trees. It came from a little cottage and they crept up to the window. The donkey placed his front hoofs on the window ledge. Anxious to see, the dog jumped on the donkey's back, the cat climbed onto the dog and the cockerel flew on top of the cat to watch what was going on inside.

Now, the cottage was the hideaway of a gang of bandits who were busily celebrating their latest robbery. The hungry donkey and his friends became excited when they saw the food on the table. Upset by

the jittery crew on his back, the donkey stuck his head through the window and toppled his three companions on to the lamp. The light went out and the room rang with the braying of the donkey who had cut his nose on the glass, the barking of the dog and the snarling of the cat. The cockerel screeched along with the others.

Taken completely by surprise, the terrified bandits fled screaming: "The Devil! The Devil!" And their abandoned meal ended up in the four friends' stomachs.

Later, however, just as the donkey and his companions were dropping off to sleep, one of the bandits crept back to the now quiet house and went in to find out what had taken place. He opened the door, and with his pistol in his hand, he stepped trembling towards the fire. However, mistaking the glow of the cat's eyes for burning coals, he thrust a candle between them and instantly the furious cat sank its claws into the bandit's face. The man fell backwards on to the dog, dropping his gun, which went off, and the animal's sharp teeth sank into his leg. When the donkey saw the bandit's figure at the door, he gave a tremendous kick, sending the man flying right through the doorway. The cockerel greeted this feat with a grim crowing sound.

"Run!" screamed the bandit. "Run! A horrible witch in there scratched my face, a demon bit me on the leg and a monster beat me with a stick! And . . ." But the other bandits were no longer listening, for they had taken to their heels and fled.

And so the donkey, the dog, the cat and the cockerel took over the house without any trouble and, with the booty left behind by the bandits, always had food on the table, and lived happy and contented for many years.

Once upon a time . . .

. . . a conceited hare challenged a long-suffering tortoise to an absurd race. And, incredible though it may seem to you, this is the story . . .

THE HARE AND THE TORTOISE

Once upon a time . . . . there was a hare who, boasting how he could run faster than anyone else, was forever teasing a tortoise for its slowness. Then one day, the irate tortoise answered back: "Who do you think you are? There's no denying you're swift, but even you can be beaten!" The hare squealed with laughter.

"Beaten in a race? By whom? Not you, surely! I bet there's nobody in the world that can win against me, I'm so speedy. Now, why don't you try?"

Annoyed by such bragging, the tortoise accepted the challenge. A course was planned, and next day at dawn they stood at the starting line. The hare yawned sleepily as the meek tortoise trudged slowly off. When the hare saw how painfully slow his rival was, he decided, half asleep on his feet, to have a quick nap. "Take your time!" he said. "I'll have forty winks and catch up with you in a minute."

The hare woke with a start from a fitful sleep and gazed round, looking for the tortoise. But the creature was only a short distance away, having barely covered a third of the course. Breathing a sigh of relief, the hare decided he might as well have breakfast too, and off he went to munch some cabbages he had noticed in a nearby field. But the heavy meal and the hot sun made his eyelids droop. With a careless glance at the tortoise, now halfway along the course, he decided to have another snooze before flashing past the winning post. And smiling at the thought of the look on the tortoise's face when it saw the hare speed by, he fell fast asleep and was soon snoring happily. The sun started to sink below the horizon, and the tortoise, who had been plodding towards the winning post since morning, was scarcely a yard from the finish. At that very point, the hare woke with a jolt. He could see the tortoise a speck in the distance and away he dashed. He leapt and bounded at a great rate, his tongue lolling, and gasping for breath. Just a little more and he'd be first at the finish. But the hare's last leap was just too late, for the tortoise had beaten him to the winning post. Poor hare! Tired and in disgrace, he slumped down beside the tortoise who was silently smiling at him.

"Slowly does it every time!" he said.

THE FOX AND THE STORK

Once upon a time . . . a fox made friends with a stork and decided to invite her to lunch. While he was wondering what to serve for the meal, he thought he'd play a trick on the bird. So he prepared a tasty soup and poured it into two flat plates.

"Help yourself, Mrs Stork! I'm sure you'll enjoy this! It's frog soup and chopped parsley. Taste it, you'll find it's delicious!"

"Thank you very much!" said the stork, sniffing the soup. But she quickly saw the trick the fox had played on her. For no matter how she tried, she could not drink the soup from the flat plate. The sniggering fox urged her on: "Eat up! Do you like it?" But all the stork could do was bluff. With a casual air she said: "I'm afraid I've such a headache that I've lost my appetite!" And the fox fussily replied: "What a shame! And it's such good soup too! Too bad! Maybe next time . . ." To which the stork quickly replied: "Yes, of course! Next time, you must have lunch with me!"

The very next day, the fox found a polite note pinned to his door: it was the stork's invitation to lunch. "Now, isn't that nice of her!" said the fox to himself. "And she hasn't taken my little trick to heart either! A real lady!"

The stork's house was much plainer than the fox's, and she apologized to the fox. "My home is much humbler than yours," she said, "but I've cooked a really special meal. Freshwater shrimps with white wine and juniper berries!" The fox licked his lips at the idea of these goodies and sniffed deeply when the stork handed him his jar. But, try as he might, he was unable to eat a bite, for he could not reach down with his nose into the long neck of the jar. In the meantime, with her long beak, the stork gobbled her lunch. "Try it! Try it!" she said. "Do you like it?" But the unlucky fox, confused and outsmarted, could not think of an excuse for not eating.

And as he tossed and turned hungrily in bed that night, thinking of his lost lunch, he said to himself with a sigh: "I might have known!"

THE COCK, THE CAT, AND THE MOUSE

Once upon a time . . . a little mouse decided to go and see the world. Packing some food for the journey, he carefully locked his door and set off for the unknown. And what a wonderful world he saw! Tall trees, rolling countryside, flowers and butterflies he had never set eyes on before. On he hiked till, tired out, he came to a peasant's cottage. After eating some of his packed lunch, he thought he would inspect what, to him, was a peculiar sort of building. He entered the farmyard and his eyes grew round as saucers: there in front of him were two strange animals he had never seen before. One was large and handsome, with four legs, covered all over with soft fur, and sporting splendid white whiskers that gave it a solemn respectable air. It was dozing against the wall. The other, a two-legged creature, had red, yellow and green feathers and a fierce, bad-tempered look. A pair of cruel eyes

202

in a red-crested head glared at the little mouse.

"How do you do, sir! How do you do . . ." began the mouse's greeting, as he felt foolish at not knowing the stranger's name. But the feathered creature simply puffed out its chest, screeched a loud "Cock-a-doodle-doo!" and strutted towards the mouse, now paralyzed with fear. The little mouse saw the big yellow beak hovering over him. "I must run!" he squeaked, turning tail and fleeing as fast as his legs would carry him. He spied a hole in the wall and dived into it. Inside, three faces stared at him in amazement.

"Where did you appear from?" they asked.

"I've come . . ." gasped the little mouse breathlessly, ". . . from far away! Where am I now?"

"This is our home. We're field mice. What happened?" And the little mouse told them about the animals he had met in the farmyard: one handsome and harmless, the other brightly coloured and ferocious.   The three field mice laughed. "Calm down," they said. "Have a cup of coffee. Don't you realize the danger you were in? The creature that frightened you is only a cock, but the nice harmless one is our deadliest enemy, the cat! If he'd seen you, you wouldn't be here to tell the tale. As you see, you can't always judge by appearances!"

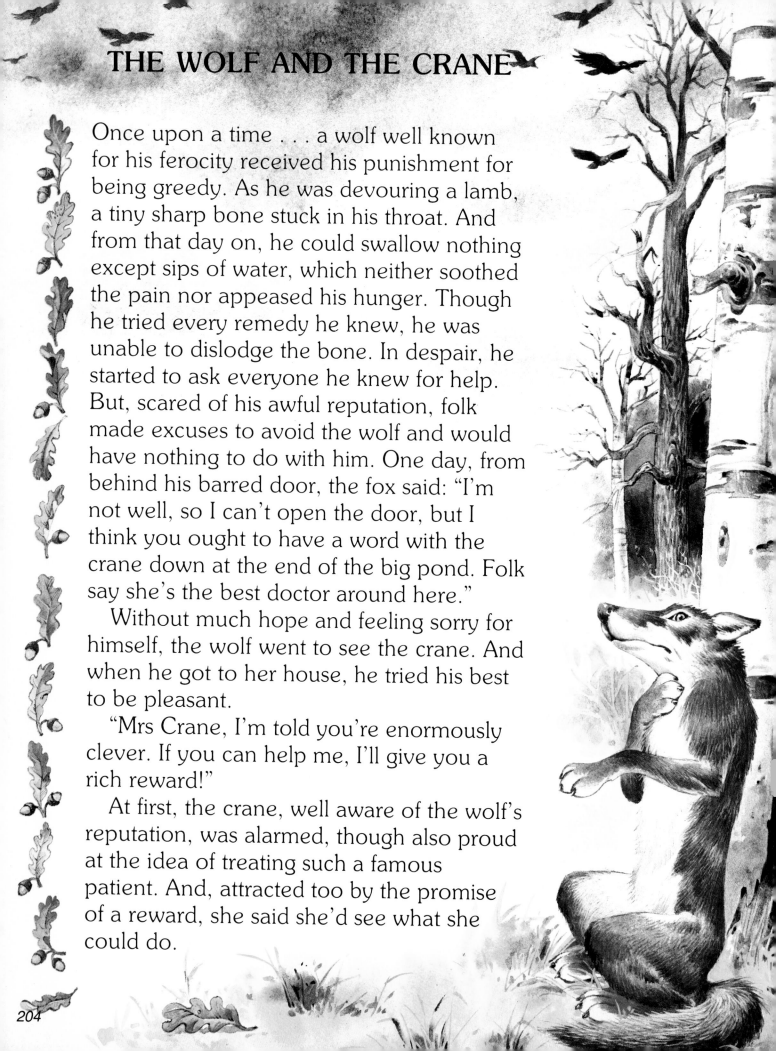

THE WOLF AND THE CRANE

Once upon a time . . . a wolf well known for his ferocity received his punishment for being greedy. As he was devouring a lamb, a tiny sharp bone stuck in his throat. And from that day on, he could swallow nothing except sips of water, which neither soothed the pain nor appeased his hunger. Though he tried every remedy he knew, he was unable to dislodge the bone. In despair, he started to ask everyone he knew for help. But, scared of his awful reputation, folk made excuses to avoid the wolf and would have nothing to do with him. One day, from behind his barred door, the fox said: "I'm not well, so I can't open the door, but I think you ought to have a word with the crane down at the end of the big pond. Folk say she's the best doctor around here."

Without much hope and feeling sorry for himself, the wolf went to see the crane. And when he got to her house, he tried his best to be pleasant.

"Mrs Crane, I'm told you're enormously clever. If you can help me, I'll give you a rich reward!"

At first, the crane, well aware of the wolf's reputation, was alarmed, though also proud at the idea of treating such a famous patient. And, attracted too by the promise of a reward, she said she'd see what she could do.

The wolf opened wide his huge mouth. The crane shuddered at the thought of peering inside the red jaws with their sharp fangs, but plucking up her courage, she said: "Now, please keep your mouth wide open, or I won't be able to remove the bone!" And she poked her long beak down the wolf's throat and pulled out the little bone.

"There! You can close your mouth again. You'll be able to swallow whatever you like now!" The wolf could hardly believe it. His throat was clear at last! Highly delighted, the crane said: "See how clever I am? You didn't feel a thing! I whipped out that nasty bone with my long beak! And as for my

reward . . ." The wolf interrupted with a scowl.

"Reward? What reward? You ought to be grateful that I didn't bite your head off while it was down my throat! You should give *me* a reward for sparing your life!"

Seeing the wolf's bloodshot eyes, the crane realized she was now in danger. What more could she expect from such a wicked wolf? And she vowed that, from then on, she'd only treat patients too harmless ever to threaten her.

THE VAIN CROW

Once upon a time . . . a restless crow decided to go farther away than usual from home and friends. Suddenly, in a farmyard, he met a pair of peacocks. What wonderful birds they were! The crow had never seen such beautiful feathers, and he timidly asked the regal-looking birds what they were.

"We're peacocks," one of them replied, spreading its tail. And as the peacock strutted about, showing the crow his magnificent feathers, he screamed, as peacocks do. Bursting with admiration, the crow said goodbye and flapped away, but as he flew home, he could not forget the two peacocks. "What fine feathers! They must be so happy, being so beautiful." And he gazed down sadly at his own ugly plumes. From that day on, he could not help thinking about the splendour of the peacocks and his own plain feathers. He even stopped looking at himself in the pond water, for every time he did so, it made him even more depressed. He got into the habit of spying on the peacocks, and the more he watched them strut royally around, the more envious he was of their beauty.

One day, he noticed that one of the peacocks had dropped a feather. When the sun went down, the crow picked it up and hid it away. For days on end, he watched the peacocks and found another feather. When he had four, he could wait no longer: he stuck the peacock feathers onto his own tail, using pine resin, and started to parade up and down for his friends to admire.

"Just look at my gorgeous tail!" he said proudly.

"I'm not ugly like you! Out of my way, you moth eaten crows!" The crows' amazement soon changed to indignation, then they started to laugh and jeer at their vain companion. "You're nothing but a crow yourself, even with those flashy feathers!" they jeered.

"And you're silly as well as ugly," replied the conceited crow haughtily, and off he went to live with the peacocks. When the peacocks set eyes on the stranger, they thought the crow was just another peacock who, for some reason, had lost most of his feathers, and they felt sorry for him. But the crow, vainer than ever, wanted to attract greater admiration and a foolish idea came into his head. He tried to scream the way the peacocks do when they fan their tails. But the harsh "Craw! Craw! Craw!" quickly betrayed the crow. The furious peacocks pecked the stolen feathers off and chased the crow away. Poor crow! For when, sad and downcast, he went back to his friends, he was given exactly the same rough treatment. Nobody would speak to him and all the crows turned their backs on him for trying to be what he was not.

THE HOLE THAT WAS TOO NARROW

Once upon a time . . . a stoat was so greedy that he would eat anything that came his way. But he was punished for his greed. He found some old stale eggs in a barn and, as usual, gobbled the lot. However, he soon started to feel agonizing pains in his tummy, his eyes grew dim and he broke out in a cold sweat. For days, he lay between life and death, then the fever dropped. The first time he dared climb a tree to rob a nest, thin and weak, with his trousers dangling over an empty stomach, he became dizzy and fell. That is how he twisted his ankle. Sick with hunger, he limped about in search of food, but that made him feel even hungrier than before. Then good luck came his way. Although wary of venturing too close to human habitations, he was so hungry he went up to a tavern on the outskirts of the village. The air was full of lovely smells and the poor stoat felt his mouth watering as he pictured all the nice things inside. An inviting smell coming from a crack in the wall seemed to be stronger than the others. Thrusting his nose into the crack, he was greeted by a waft of delicious scents. The stoat frantically clawed at the crack with his paws and teeth, trying to widen it. Slowly the plaster between the blocks of rubble began to crumble, till all he had to do was move a stone. Shoving with all his might, the stoat made a hole. And then a *really* wonderful sight met his gaze. He was inside the pantry, where hams, salamis, cheeses, honey, jam and nuts were stored. Overwhelmed by it all, the stoat could

not make up his mind what to taste first. He jumped from one thing to another, munching all the time, till his tummy was full. Satisfied at last, he fell asleep. Then he woke again, had another feast and went back to sleep. With all this food, his strength returned, and next day, the stoat was strong enough to climb up to the topmost shelves and select the tastiest delicacies. By this time, he was just having a nibble here and a nibble there. But he never stopped eating: he went on and on and on. By now, he was very full indeed, as he chattered to himself: "Salami for starters . . . no, the ham's better! Some soft cheese and a spot of mature cheese as well . . . I think I'll have a pickled sausage too . . ."

In only a few days, the stoat had become very fat and his trouser button had popped off over a bulging tummy. But of course, the stoat's fantastic luck could not last for ever.

One afternoon, the stoat froze in mid-munch at the creak of a door. Heavy footsteps thumped down the stairs, and the stoat looked helplessly round. Fear of discovery sent him hunting for a way to escape. He ran towards the hole in the wall through which he had come. But though his head and shoulders entered the hole, his tummy, which had grown much larger since the day he had come in, simply would not pass. The stoat was in a dangerous position: he was stuck! Two thick hands grabbed him by the tail.

"You horrid little robber! So you thought you'd get away, did you? I'll soon deal with you!"

Strange though it may sound, the only thought in the greedy stoat's head was a longing to be starving of hunger again . . .

THE WOLF AND THE LAMB

Once upon a time . . . in the forest lived a wolf, known to be savage and ruthless. One day, feeling thirsty, the wolf went down to a stream, and as he drank the sparkling water, he saw a lamb drinking, further downstream. The minute he set eyes on the hapless lamb, he decided to make a meal of it. "A nice plump lamb! Fine and tender! Yummy! That will be delicious! I haven't had such luck in ages! Now, I must find an excuse for picking a quarrel, so that nobody can accuse me of gobbling it unjustly!"

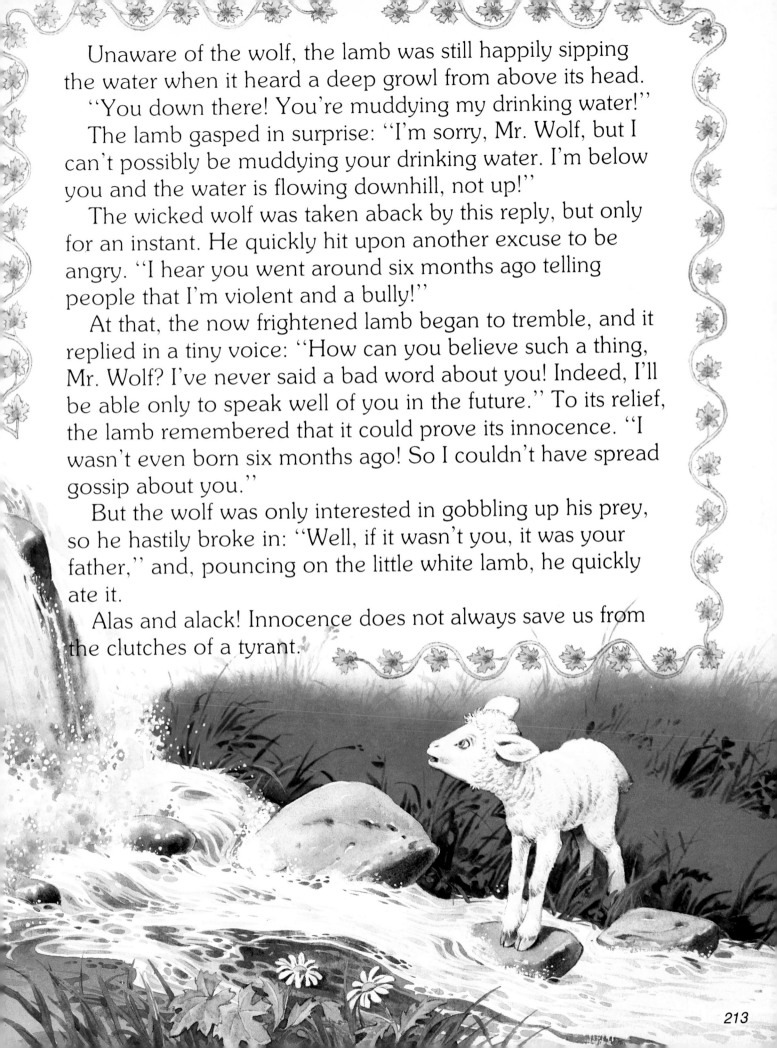

Unaware of the wolf, the lamb was still happily sipping the water when it heard a deep growl from above its head.

"You down there! You're muddying my drinking water!"

The lamb gasped in surprise: "I'm sorry, Mr. Wolf, but I can't possibly be muddying your drinking water. I'm below you and the water is flowing downhill, not up!"

The wicked wolf was taken aback by this reply, but only for an instant. He quickly hit upon another excuse to be angry. "I hear you went around six months ago telling people that I'm violent and a bully!"

At that, the now frightened lamb began to tremble, and it replied in a tiny voice: "How can you believe such a thing, Mr. Wolf? I've never said a bad word about you! Indeed, I'll be able only to speak well of you in the future." To its relief, the lamb remembered that it could prove its innocence. "I wasn't even born six months ago! So I couldn't have spread gossip about you."

But the wolf was only interested in gobbling up his prey, so he hastily broke in: "Well, if it wasn't you, it was your father," and, pouncing on the little white lamb, he quickly ate it.

Alas and alack! Innocence does not always save us from the clutches of a tyrant.

THE MONKEY KING

Once upon a time . . . a long time
ago, there was a thick jungle
where many kinds of animals lived
in harmony together. Their ruler
was a wise old lion. But one sad
day, the king died and the animals
had to decide who was to be their new ruler. The dead king
had a gold crown, encrusted with precious gems, and it was
decided that all the candidates for the throne were to come
forward and each would try on the crown, and the ruler
would be the animal whose head it fitted. Now, though many
tried on the crown, it fitted no one. Some heads were too big,
others too small, a few had horns and some had big ears. The
fact was that the old king's crown did not fit any of the
animals. Then a cheeky monkey snatched up the crown and
started to amuse the crowd with clever tricks. First, he slipped
the crown round his waist and whirled it round and round his
middle without letting it fall to the ground. Then he
tossed it higher and higher into the air and caught it as
it came down. He then stood on his head and twirled
the crown on the tips of his toes, before jumping to
his feet again and catching it in his hands. All the
animals laughed delightedly at the nimble monkey's
skill and clapped in excitement. Pleased at the great
applause, the monkey went on with his show, till
the enthusiastic crowd decided to award him the
crown and proclaim him king.
　　　　The only animal to disagree was the fox.
"A silly creature like that can't be our king!"
he said. "I'm going to do all I can to make
him lose the throne."

214

One day, having just managed to avoid a trap that men had set at the edge of the jungle, the fox took it unseen to the tree where the monkey lived. Covering the trap with dead leaves, the fox picked a large bunch of bananas and called up to the monkey: "Sire! Sire! Can you help me? I have some ripe bananas I'd like to present you with, but I can't climb trees as easily as you do! Would you please come down and accept my gift?" The unsuspecting monkey shinned down the tree, and just as he reached for the bananas, the trap suddenly clamped shut over his legs. The fox began to laugh: "What a foolish king we have! Fancy falling into a trap for a handful of bananas!" And calling all the other animals, he went on: "Just look at our sovereign! Isn't he stupid? He can't even avoid being caught in a trap. If he isn't able to watch out for himself, how can we expect him to look after us?" All the animals let themselves be persuaded by the fox's words, and in a twinkling the monkey king was deprived of the crown. And from that day on, this particular jungle was the only one whose animals made do without a king.

THE FOX AND THE GRAPES

Once upon a time . . . in a wood there lived a very crafty quick-witted fox. The rabbits, rats, the birds and all the other creatures fled at the sight of him, for they all knew how cruel and famished he was. And since his prey kept fearfully out of sight, the fox had no choice but to haunt the neighbourhood buildings in the hope of finding something to eat. The first time, he was in luck. Near a lonely peasant's cottage, only a low fence stood between him and the hen run, and there he left death and destruction behind him.

"What careless men, leaving such tender fat hens unguarded," he said to himself as he trotted away, still munching.

A few days later, hungry once more, he decided to visit the same hen run again. He crept up to the fence. A thread of smoke curled from the cottage chimney, but all was quiet. With a great bound, he leapt into the hen run. The cackling hens scattered, and the fox was already clutching one in his jaws when a stone hit him on the side.

"Wicked brute!" yelled a man waving a stick. "Now I've got you!"

To make matters worse, up raced a large dog, snarling viciously. The fox dropped the hen and tried to jump out of the

hen run. At the first try, he fell back, perhaps weak with fright. He could almost feel the dog's fangs sink into his ear, but with a desperate jump, he got over the fence. The yells and stones streamed after the bruised fox as he ran into the wood. In a nearby glade, he glanced round to make sure that he was not being followed. "Bad luck!" he said to himself. "All those hens . . ." His mouth was watering and he could feel gnawing hunger pains. Right above his head stretched a vine, laden with bunches of big ripe grapes. "Well, if there's nothing else . . ." muttered the fox, jumping up towards the grapes. But the bunches were hanging just beyond his reach. The fox then took a running jump at them, but without success. And though he tried over and over again, the grapes remained beyond his grasp.

"Craw! Craw! Craw!" laughed a crow overhead, mocking the disappointed fox.

"Sour grapes!" exclaimed the fox loudly. 'I'll come back when they're ripe." And thrusting out his chest to give himself airs, though still smarting from the blows he had received, he set off towards the woods with an empty stomach.

THE ANT AND THE CRICKET

Once upon a time . . . one hot summer, a cricket sang cheerfully on the branch of a tree, while down below, a long line of ants struggled gamely under the weight of their load of grains; and between one song and the next, the cricket spoke to the ants. "Why are you working so hard? Come into the shade, away from the sun, and sing a song with me." But the tireless ants went on with their work . . . "We can't do that," they said. "We must store away food for the winter. When the weather's cold and the ground white with snow, there's nothing to eat, and we'll survive the winter only if the pantry is full."

"There's plenty of summer to come," replied the cricket, "and lots of time to fill the pantry before winter. I'd rather sing! How can anyone work in this heat and sun?"

And so, all summer, the cricket sang while the ants laboured. But the days turned into weeks and the weeks into months. Autumn came, the leaves began to fall and the

cricket left the bare tree. The grass too was turning thin and yellow. One morning, the cricket woke shivering with cold. An early frost tinged the fields with white and turned the last of the green leaves brown: winter had come at last. The cricket wandered, feeding on the few dry stalks left on the hard frozen ground. Then the snow fell and she could find nothing at all to eat. Trembling and famished, she thought sadly of the warmth and her summer songs. One evening, she saw a speck of light in the distance, and trampling through the thick snow, made her way towards it.

"Open the door! Please open the door! I'm starving! Give me some food!" An ant leant out of the window.

"Who's there? Who is it?"

"It's me – the cricket. I'm cold and hungry, with no roof over my head."

"The cricket? Ah, yes! I remember you. And what were *you* doing all summer while we were getting ready for winter?"

"Me? I was singing and filling the whole earth and sky with my song!"

"Singing, eh?" said the ant. "Well, try dancing now!"

THE HORSE AND THE DONKEY

Once upon a time . . . an old carter kept a horse and a donkey in the same stable. He was equally fond of both his animals, but as he used the horse to pull his trap, he gave it better food and more attention than he did the donkey. However, the donkey, knowing he was not so precious as his stablemate, ate straw instead of corn and hay, without complaining. Even when both animals carried sacks to market, the donkey's was the heavier load, for the carter did not want to overwork his noble horse, though he had no such feelings about the donkey. As time went by, the horse grew more handsome and robust, while the donkey became thin and weak. One day, on their way to market, the donkey was carrying his usual heavy load, while the horse had only two lightweight sacks tied to the saddle.

"I can't go much further!" moaned the donkey. "I'm much weaker today! I can hardly stand and unless I can get rid of some of this weight, I won't be able to go on. Couldn't you take some of my load?"

When the horse heard this, he looked the donkey up and down in disdain, for he considered himself much superior, and said: "Our master gave you the heavy load, because he knows that donkeys are beasts of burden. Their loads ought to be heavier than those of noble horses!"

So the wretched donkey stumbled on. But after a short distance, he stopped again, bleary-eyed, his tongue hanging out.

"Please, please listen! If you don't help me, I'll never reach market alive." But without even a glance, the horse haughtily replied: "Rubbish! Come on, you'll manage this time too!"

But this time, after a few tottering steps, the donkey dropped dead to the ground. The donkey's master, who had lingered to pick mushrooms, ran up when he saw the animal fall.

"Poor thing!" he said. "He served me well for so many years. His load must have been too heavy."

Then he turned to the horse: "Come here! You'll have to carry your companion's load too now!" And he hoisted the donkey's sacks onto the horse's back.

"I'd have done better to help the donkey when he was alive," said the horse to himself. "A little more weight wouldn't have done me any harm. Now, I'm frightened of collapsing myself under a double load!" But feeling sorry too late did nothing to lighten his load.

THE LION GOES TO WAR

Once upon a time . . . a lion decided to go to war. He summoned his ministers, and called together his army with this proclamation: "King Lion commands that all animals in the forest must come before him tomorrow to go to war. Nobody must fail to appear."

The lion's subjects all presented themselves punctually and the lion issued the orders: "Elephant, you're the largest, you'll transport the guns and all the supplies. You, fox, have a reputation for cunning, so you'll help me draw up the plans of battle to beat off enemy attacks. You, monkey, nimble and good at climbing trees, will act as lookout and spy the enemy's movements from above. Bear, you're strong and agile, so you'll scale the fortress walls and terrorize the enemy."

Amongst those present were also the rabbit and the donkey. When the king's ministers saw them, they shook their heads, then one said: "Sire, I don't think the donkey will make a good soldier. They say he's easily frightened."

The lion looked at the donkey, then turning to his ministers, he remarked:

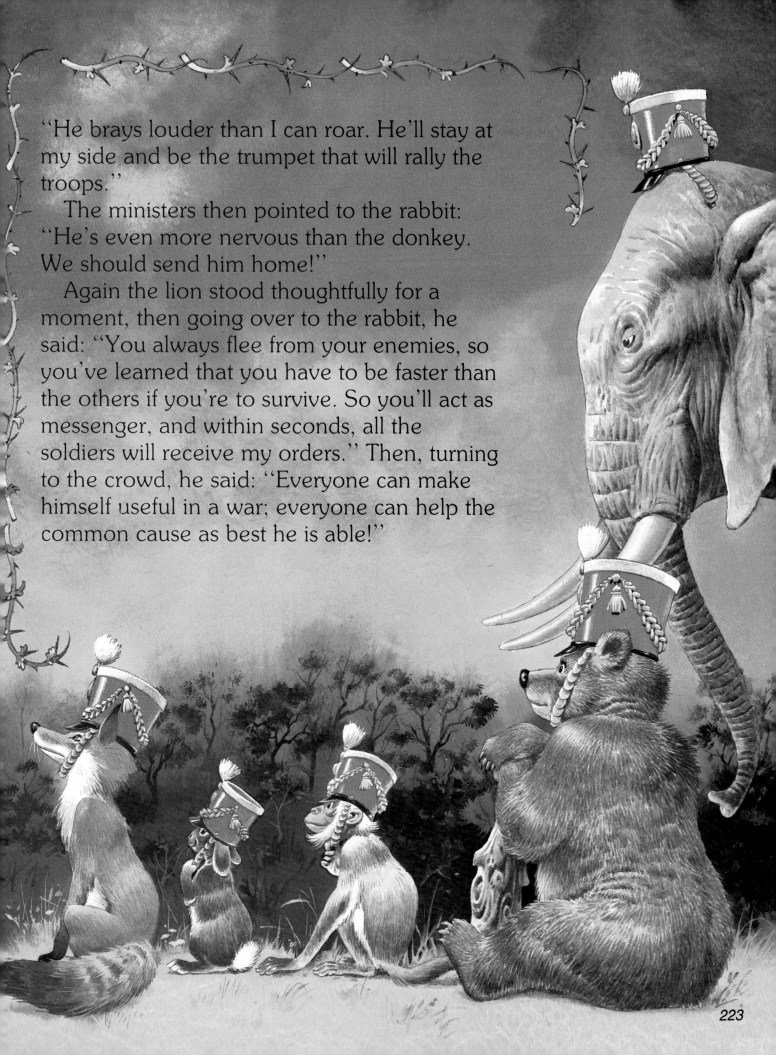

"He brays louder than I can roar. He'll stay at my side and be the trumpet that will rally the troops."

The ministers then pointed to the rabbit: "He's even more nervous than the donkey. We should send him home!"

Again the lion stood thoughtfully for a moment, then going over to the rabbit, he said: "You always flee from your enemies, so you've learned that you have to be faster than the others if you're to survive. So you'll act as messenger, and within seconds, all the soldiers will receive my orders." Then, turning to the crowd, he said: "Everyone can make himself useful in a war; everyone can help the common cause as best he is able!"

THE CONCEITED STAG

Once upon a time . . . there was a stag with splendidly long antlers, who was very conceited. Every time he drank at a pool, he would stand and admire his reflection in the water. "I am handsome," he would tell himself. "There's no finer set of antlers in the forest!" And off he would prance. Like all stags, he had long slender legs, but folk said he'd rather break a leg than lose a single branch of his splendid antlers. Poor foolish stag! How vain he was.

One day, as he grazed peacefully on the tender shoots on some low branches, he heard a distant shot.

He heard with fear the baying of the hounds. Terrified, he knew what terrible enemies the hounds were and that, if they caught his scent, it would not be easy to outrun them.

He had to flee, at once, and as quickly as possible. Faster and faster, he sped along the woodland track, his heart in his mouth. He could hear the baying of the pack at his heels. Without ever looking back, he ran in a straight line, trying to shake off his pursuers. Then the wood thinned out into a clearing. "With luck, I'll be safe now," he said to himself, running swiftly over the smooth ground. And indeed, the yelping of the hounds seemed to die away in the distance.

Only a little further now, and the stag would reach safety. Suddenly, as he swept under a tree, his antlers caught in the low-hanging branches. He shook his head desperately, trying to break free, but although he struggled, his antlers were held fast. The hounds were coming closer and closer. Just before the stag met his doom, he had time to think: "What a mistake I made in regarding my antlers as the best and most precious part of my body. I should have had more respect for my legs. They tried to carry me to safety, while my antlers will be the death of me!"

THE HORSE AND THE WOLF

Once upon a time . . . a horse was grazing peacefully in a rolling green meadow. A famished wolf passing by saw the horse and his mouth began to water.

"That's a fine horse! And will taste good too! He'd make a juicy steak! Pity he's so big, I don't think I'd manage to bring him down, though you never know . . ."

The wolf approached the horse, which continued to eat the grass. ". . . maybe, if I take him by surprise."

Now quite close, the wolf spoke to the horse, trying to sound as pleasant as he could.

"Good day, Mr. Horse, I see you're enjoying a meal. Is the grass good? I must say you're looking rather pale. Aren't you well?"

His mouth full of grass, the horse replied: "Pale? Oh, no, that's my natural colour. I was born white and grey."

The wolf pretended not to understand what the horse had said. "Yes, indeed, very pale. It's just as well your master has given you a holiday in the field, instead of working."

"A holiday in the field? But I'm the picture of health! . . ."

The wolf was now circling round the horse, trying to find the best point of attack.

"I'm a doctor," he went on. "I can treat you. If you tell me where the pain is, I'm sure I can cure it. Take my advice. Let me examine you!"

The horse, who was not usually wary of others, became suspicious of the wolf's persistent remarks, and thought he had better be on his guard. The wolf was now very close and carefully biding his time, when the horse said, in alarm: "Yes! Now that I think of it, I have a sore hind foot. It's been swollen for ages . . ."

Without a moment's thought, the wolf trotted up to the hoof which the horse had obligingly raised into the air. And when he was certain that the wolf had come within range, the horse gave a mighty kick, catching the wolf on the jawbone and sending him flying.

"Would you like to examine me again?" The wolf heard the words as he struggled to his feet with spinning head.

"No thanks! That's enough for one day!" he mumbled, limping away, with no further thought for horse steaks.

THE OX AND THE FROG

Once upon a time . . . a conceited frog never missed an opportunity to show his friends how different he was, and how much better than everyone else. When folk were jumping, he always tried to do the highest jump, when it was a question of diving, he was first into the water. In other words, he had to be tops all the time. One day, a big ox came to drink at the pond. Frightened, all the frogs hopped away to hide in the reeds, but when they saw that the ox was harmless, they came out again to watch the huge beast. "Isn't he whopping!" they exclaimed to each other. One frog then said: "It would take hundreds of frogs like us to make one of him!"

Now, the conceited frog, far more scared than the others, had dived into the water at the sight of the ox. But a little later he returned and, after listening to his friends' remarks, he said: "He's certainly bigger than we are. But he's not *enormous*!"

But nobody was paying any attention to the conceited frog, so he raised his voice . . . and puffing out his chest, announced: "I could easily become as big as that ox! Look!"

The frogs began to smirk. "You're very little, far too little!" But the frog just blew himself out even more. "Now look," he whispered, as he tried not to lose air. His friends giggled. "What about now?" he managed to gasp, as he blew some more. "The ox is much bigger," came the reply. The conceited frog made a last great effort: taking an extra deep breath, he blew himself up until . . . BANG! His skin burst! The astonished frogs saw their friend disappear from sight, for nothing was left of the conceited frog but scraps of green skin. The ox, who had raised his head when he heard the bang, went back to his drinking, and the frogs hopped away, remarking: "It doesn't do to become too swollen-headed . . ."

THE GREEDY DOG

Once upon a time . . . a dog managed to steal a
large steak from a butcher's shop, and ran into the
woods to eat it in peace. On reaching the banks of
a stream, he happened to see his face reflected in
the water. Never for a moment thinking that he
was looking at himself in the water, what he
thought he saw was another dog, holding a large
steak in its mouth.

Being a greedy dog, he jumped into the stream
to snatch the other dog's meat. Of course, the
reflection vanished and he could see no sign of
dog or steak.

Only then did he realize that, when he barked to
frighten the other, he had dropped his stolen meat.
Unluckily for him, the current was swift and the
steak had been carried away. And though the dog
hunted all over, he couldn't find a trace of it.
Which meant, that instead of having two steaks, he
was left with nothing.

THE OBSTINATE GOATS

Once upon a time . . . two mountain goats happened to be going down the opposite slopes of a valley, through which flowed a rushing river.

Now, some of the mountain dwellers had bridged the river by placing a large tree trunk that had been struck by lightning, to join the steep rocky banks.

The two goats met head on half way across the tree trunk for each wanted to cross to the other side. But the trunk was not nearly wide enough for them to pass each other, and neither goat was inclined to give way. Obstinately, they began to bicker, but neither would budge an inch. Words soon led to action and they started to fight, till finally both tumbled off the tree trunk into the river below. Wouldn't it have been much simpler if only one of the goats had been courteous enough to allow the other to pass?

THE LION AND THE MOSQUITO

Once upon a time . . . a tiny mosquito started to buzz round a lion he met. "Go away!" grumbled the sleepy lion, smacking his own cheek in an attempt to drive the insect away.

"Why should I?" demanded the mosquito. "You're king of the jungle, not of the air! I'll fly wherever I want and land wherever I please." And so saying, he tickled the lion's ear. In the hope of crushing the insect, the lion boxed his own ears, but the mosquito slipped away from the now dazed lion.

"I don't feel it any more. Either it's squashed or it's gone away." But at that very moment, the irritating buzz began again, and the mosquito flew into the lion's nose. Wild with rage, the lion leapt to his hind legs and started to rain punches on his own nose. But the insect, safe inside, refused to budge. With a swollen nose and watery eyes, the lion gave a terrific sneeze, blasting the mosquito out. Angry at being dislodged so abruptly, the mosquito returned to the attack: BUZZ . . . BUZZZ! . . . it whizzed round the lion's head. Large and tough as the lion was, he could not rid himself of his tiny tormenter. This made him angrier still, and he roared fiercely. At the sound of his terrible voice, all the forest creatures fled in fear, but paying no heed to the exhausted lion, the mosquito said triumphantly: "There you are, king of the jungle! Foiled by a tiny mosquito like me!" And highly delighted with his victory, off he buzzed. But he did not notice a spider's web hanging close by, and soon he was turning and twisting, trying to escape from the trap set by a large spider. "Bah!" said the spider in disgust, as he ate it. "Another tiny mosquito. Not much to get excited about, but better than nothing. I was hoping for something more substantial . . ."

And that's what became of the mosquito that foiled the lion!

THE FOX AND THE CROW

Once upon a time . . . a big crow stole a lump of cheese and went to perch on a branch of a tree to eat it in peace. A passing fox sniffed the air and stopped below the tree, his mouth watering.

"Cheese?" he said. "Mmm. I'd love . . . if only I could . . ." he said to himself, greedily, wondering how to get hold of the morsel.

After a moment or two, he spoke to the crow: "You *are* a fine crow! I've never seen anyone so big and strong. What lovely thick shiny feathers you have! And such slender legs, the sign of a noble bird. And a regal beak. That's it: the beak of a king! You ought to be crowned King of the Birds!"

When the crow heard such glowing praise of his beauty, he stretched to his full length and triumphantly flapped his wings.

In his softest voice, the fox went on: "What lovely eyes you have. You don't seem to have a single fault! You're quite perfect." The crow had never been flattered so much in all his life. "Though I haven't heard your voice yet," went on the fox, "I expect that such a perfect creature like yourself can have nothing less than a wonderful singing voice!"

The crow had, till then, been blissfully drinking in the fox's praise, but he felt a prick of doubt at the sweet words about his voice. He had never heard that crows were fine singers! Of course, being a very fine crow, perhaps that meant he had a beautiful voice as well. The fox could be right! And the crow gazed down at the fox as he said: "Now then, King of the Birds, let me hear a sweet song . . ."

Throwing caution to the winds, the crow opened his beak and, taking a deep breath, loudly cawed: "Cra, Cra, Cra!" The lump of cheese fell through the air and the fox caught it neatly in his jaws. "I deserved that!" he told himself as he enjoyed the titbit. Then, licking his lips, he again spoke to the crow on the branch.

"Silly crow. You're the ugliest bird I've ever seen, you have the worst voice I've ever heard, but most of all, you're the most stupid bird I've ever met! And thanks for the cheese." And off he trotted well satisfied with himself . . .

THE MOUSE AND THE LION

Once upon a time . . . a little mouse, scampering over a lion he had chanced upon, happened to wake him up. The angry lion grabbed the mouse and held it to his jaws. "Don't eat me, Your Majesty!" the mouse pleaded: "Forgive me! If you let me go, I'll never bother you again. I'll always be grateful, and will do you a good turn one day."

The lion, who had no intention of eating such a little scrap, and only wanted to frighten the mouse, chuckled: "Well, well. A mouse that hopes to do a lion a good turn! By helping me to hunt, maybe? Or would you rather roar in my place?" The mouse was at a loss for words. "Sire, I really . . ."

"All right. You can go," said the lion, shortly, opening his paw. The mouse scurried thankfully away.

Some days later, the lion fell into a trap and found he was caught fast in a stout net. Try as he might, he could not escape. And the more he struggled, the more he became entangled in the mesh, till even his paws were held fast. He could not move an inch: it was the end. His strength, claws and fearsome fangs gave him no help in freeing himself from the tangle. He was about to resign himself to a cruel fate when he heard a small voice: "Do you need help, Sire?"

Exhausted by his struggles, his eyes wet with rage, the lion looked round. "Oh, it's you! I'm afraid there's little you can do for me . . ."

But the mouse broke in: "I can gnaw the ropes. I have strong teeth and, though it will take me some time, I'll manage." So the little mouse quickly gnawed at the meshes and soon the lion tugged a paw free, then another, till he finally succeeded in working himself free of the net.

"You see, Sire," said the mouse, "I've done you a good turn in exchange for the favour you did me in letting me go unharmed."

"How right you are. Never before has a big animal like myself had to be so grateful to a little scrap like you!"

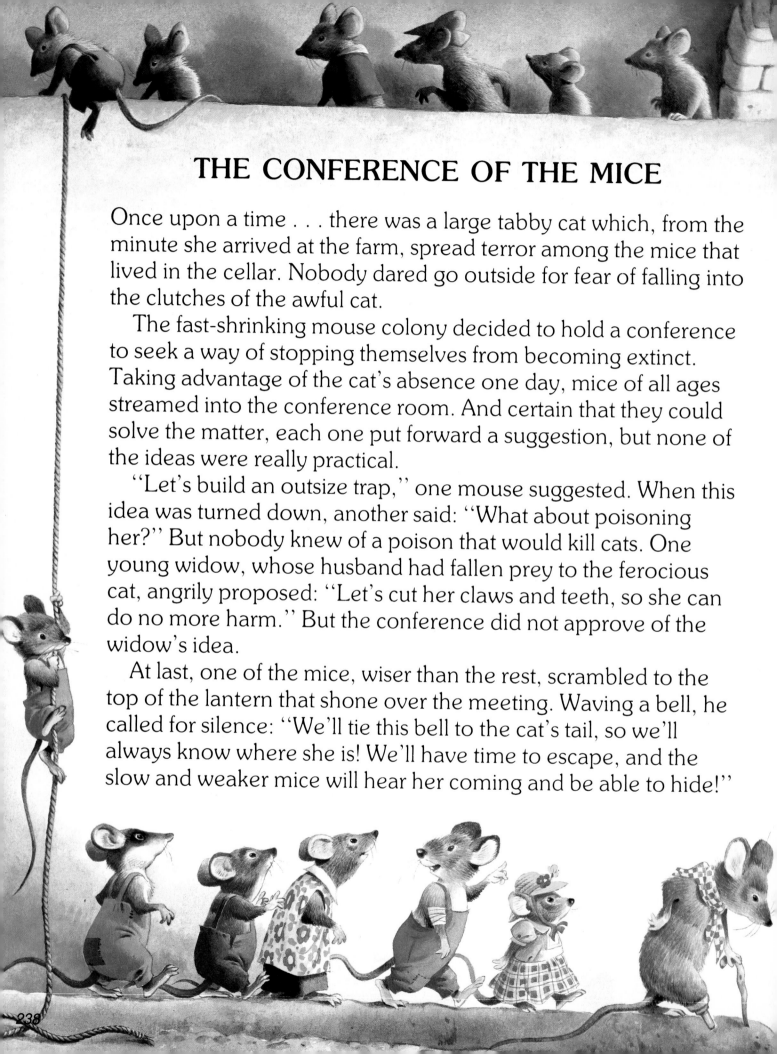

THE CONFERENCE OF THE MICE

Once upon a time . . . there was a large tabby cat which, from the minute she arrived at the farm, spread terror among the mice that lived in the cellar. Nobody dared go outside for fear of falling into the clutches of the awful cat.

The fast-shrinking mouse colony decided to hold a conference to seek a way of stopping themselves from becoming extinct. Taking advantage of the cat's absence one day, mice of all ages streamed into the conference room. And certain that they could solve the matter, each one put forward a suggestion, but none of the ideas were really practical.

"Let's build an outsize trap," one mouse suggested. When this idea was turned down, another said: "What about poisoning her?" But nobody knew of a poison that would kill cats. One young widow, whose husband had fallen prey to the ferocious cat, angrily proposed: "Let's cut her claws and teeth, so she can do no more harm." But the conference did not approve of the widow's idea.

At last, one of the mice, wiser than the rest, scrambled to the top of the lantern that shone over the meeting. Waving a bell, he called for silence: "We'll tie this bell to the cat's tail, so we'll always know where she is! We'll have time to escape, and the slow and weaker mice will hear her coming and be able to hide!"

A round of hearty applause met the wise mouse's words, and everyone congratulated him on his original idea.

". . . We'll tie it so tightly that it will never come off!"

". . . She'll never be able to sneak quietly up on us again! Why, the other day, she suddenly loomed up right in front of me! Just imagine . . ."

However, the wise mouse rang the bell again for silence. "We must decide who is going to tie the bell on the cat's tail," he said. There was not a sound in the room except for a faint murmur: "I can't, because . . ."

"Not me!" "I'd do it willingly, but . . ." "Neither can I . . ." "Not me!" "Not me!"

Nobody was brave enough to come forward to put the plan into action, and the conference of the mice ended without any decision being made. It's often very easy to have bright ideas, but putting them into practice is a more difficult matter . . .

THE DONKEY THAT THOUGHT HE WAS CLEVER

Once upon a time . . . a donkey thought he was very clever. Every day, his master harnessed him to a cart loaded with goods. They always went the same way to the village: along a wide path through the wood, down a gentle slope into farmland, then along the river to the ford and over the plain to the village.

Since the route was always the same, the donkey's master had got into the habit of having a snooze on top of the cart, while the donkey, who knew the way by heart, plodded on.

Feeling unwell one day, the man decided to risk sending the donkey by himself, with a load for urgent delivery. When the animal returned, he was given a double ration of oats as a reward.

"Since you're so clever at remembering the way," the man said, "I'm going to send you alone always, then I can do other jobs!" And from then on, in all kinds of weather, the donkey travelled to the village by himself. His master was delighted.

However, one morning, when the donkey reached the river, he decided to shorten his journey by wading across the water. But he entered the river at a deep spot, much deeper than the donkey expected, and he had to swim against the current.

Luckily, he was carrying a load of salt that day, and some of it dissolved in the water, easing the donkey's load, so that he reached the other side without much difficulty. "I am clever," said the donkey, pleased with himself. "I've found a short cut."

Next day, the man loaded the cart with sponges, and the donkey set off as usual. When he arrived at the river, he again thought he would take the short cut, and entered the water as he had done the day before. But this time, the sponges soaked up the water and made the cart heavy, so that the poor animal could not keep his head above water. And in spite of all his efforts, the donkey that thought he was so clever, sank below the surface of the water together with his load.

THE ANIMALS AND THE PLAGUE

Once upon a time . . . a terrible scourge swept through a huge forest, full of animals. It was the plague. One after the other, all the animals, big and small, strong and weak, died of the dreadful disease. None could hope to escape such a horrible fate, not even the lion himself, king of the forest. Indeed, it was the lion who gathered together the survivors, and said in a trembling voice: "This disaster is a punishment for our wicked ways. And I for one will admit I've been wicked. If you find me guilty, I'll gladly give up my life if you think that would help you in making amends for your own sins. So I confess that, during my lifetime, I've eaten many an innocent sheep."

"But, Sire," broke in one of the animals, "surely you don't think that eating sheep is a serious sin. We too . . . we too . . ." And they all began to tell their own stories.

One by one, the animals told of their crimes against their neighbours. The leopard had killed on more than one occasion, the eagle had snatched rabbits and lambs, the fox and the wolf had stolen and murdered. Even the placid-looking owl had little birds and mice on his conscience. Everyone had some wicked deed, serious or otherwise, to confess. But each animal, after his confession, was forgiven by the others, all just as guilty, of course. Last came the donkey, who said with a mortified air: "I did a very wicked thing too. One day, instead of just grazing here and there, I ate two clumps of grass in a clover meadow, without permission. I was sorry afterwards, and I've had a guilty conscience about it ever since!"

All the animals glared at the donkey and, shouting and calling insults, they chorussed: "So that's who brought the plague on us! Stealing grass from a poor peasant! Shame on you!" And the fate of the donkey was decided unanimously.

How often are innocent folk made to pay for the wicked deeds of the guilty.

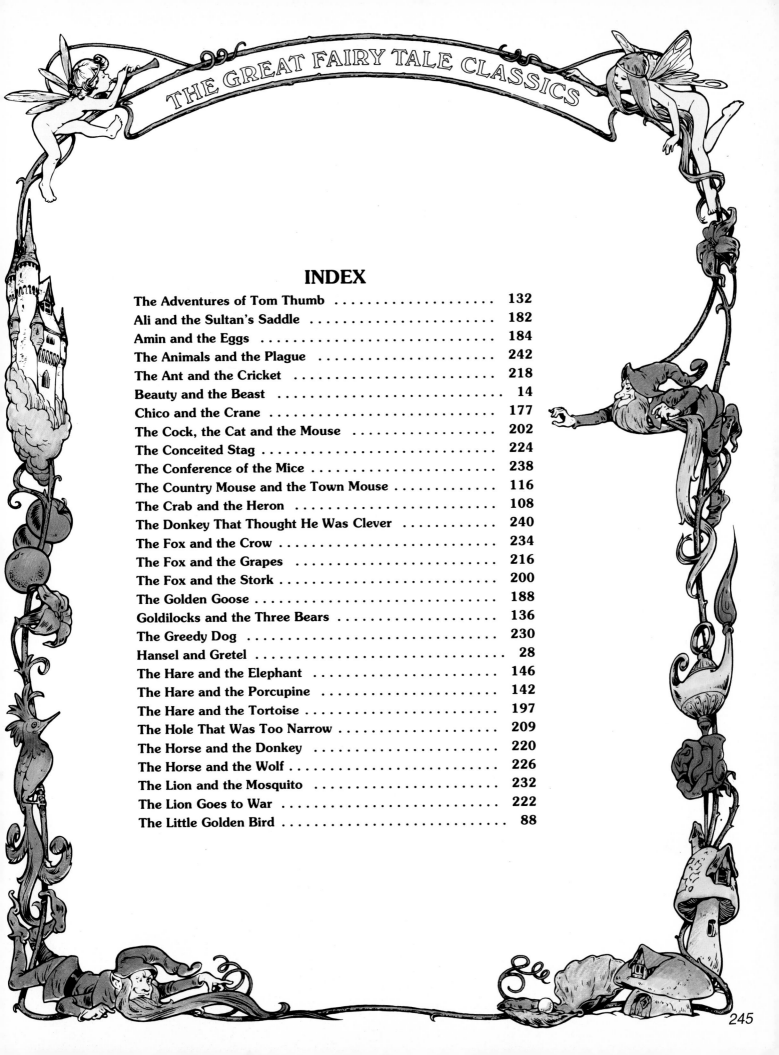

INDEX

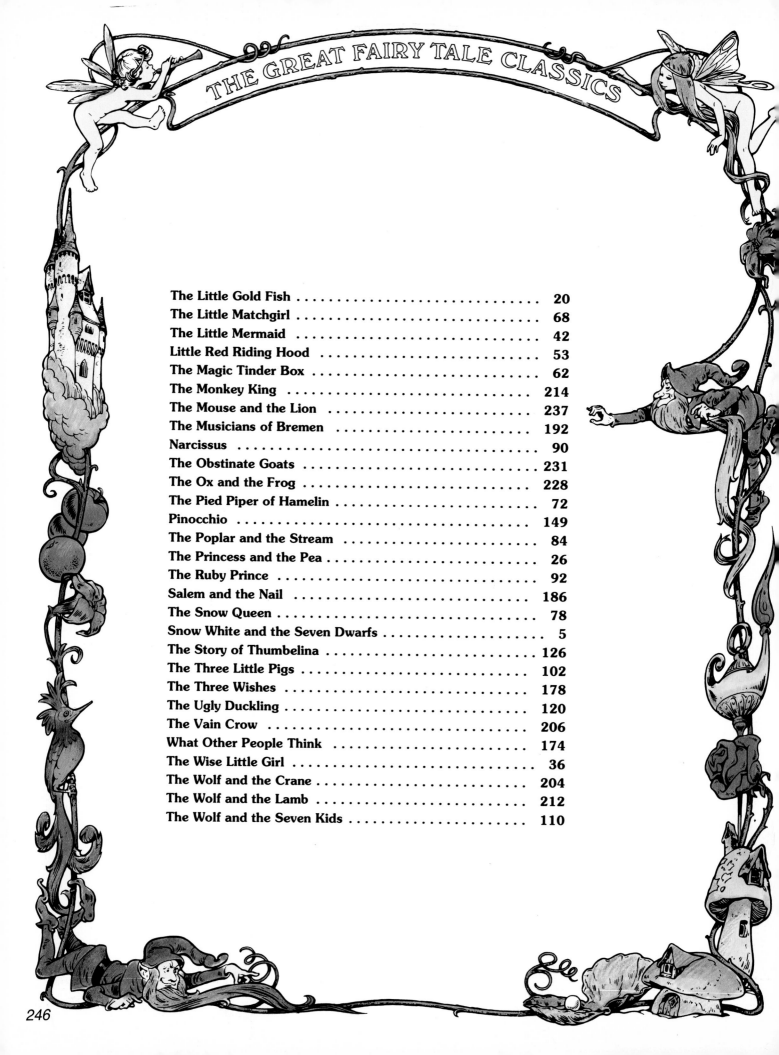

THE GREAT FAIRY TALE CLASSICS

Other tales in this series
VOL. II

CINDERELLA
BLUEBEARD
THE ADVENTURES OF ALLADIN
ALI BABA AND THE FORTY THIEVES
PUSS IN BOOTS
THE SLEEPING PRINCESS
SINBAD THE SAILOR
PRINCE OMAR AND PRINCESS SHEHERAZADE
THE TIN SOLDIER
THE ELVES AND THE SHOEMAKER
JACK AND THE BEANSTALK
THE EMPEROR'S NEW CLOTHES

and many, many more...